SHE RUNS AWAY

AN ARTEMIS BLYTHE MYSTERY THRILLER

GEORGIA WAGNER

Text Copyright © 2023 Georgia Wagner

Publisher: Greenfield Press Ltd

The right of Georgia Wagner to be identified as author of the Work has been asserted in accordance with the Copyright, Designs and Patents Act 1988

All rights reserved.

The book is copyright material and must not be copied, reproduced, transferred, distributed, leased, licensed or publicly performed or used in any way except as specifically permitted in writing by the publishers, as allowed under the terms and conditions under which it was purchased or as strictly permitted by applicable copyright law. Any unauthorised distribution or use of this text may be a direct infringement of the author's and publisher's rights and those responsible may be liable in law accordingly.

'She Runs Away' is a work of fiction. Names, characters, businesses, organisations, places, events, and incidents either are the product of the author's imagination or are used fictitiously. Any resemblance to actual persons, living or dead, and events or locations is entirely coincidental.

Contents

1. Prologue: 1
2. Chapter 1 11
3. Chapter 2 24
4. Chapter 3 33
5. Chapter 4 42
6. Chapter 5 49
7. Chapter 6 61
8. Chapter 7 69
9. Chapter 8 75
10. Chapter 9 81
11. Chapter 10 89
12. Chapter 11 103
13. Chapter 12 109

14.	Chapter 13	121
15.	Chapter 14	131
16.	Chapter 15	142
17.	Chapter 16	155
18.	Chapter 17	164
19.	Chapter 18	173
20.	Chapter 19	181
21.	Chapter 20	195
22.	Chapter 21	202
23.	What is next for Artemis Blythe?	215
24.	Also by Georgia Wagner	217
25.	Want to know more?	219
26.	About the Author	221
27.	More Books by Steve Higgs	222

PROLOGUE:

20 years before...

The artist worked, and the muse wept.

To the sound of tears, the acrylic paint streaked the canvas in slow motions. The faint scent of the paint lingered in the small, windowless room.

"Chin up, please," the painter said softly, his eyes roving from his work to the muse in the seat.

The young, brunette woman shifted uncomfortably. The wooden chair creaked with the motion, and her fingers fiddled with the arm rests. She let out a fluttering little sigh, shifting again and trying to find a comfortable position.

Her eyes kept roaming towards the door, desperate. The man at the easel sighed, lowering his paint brush briefly, and resting it over the top of a tainted water glass. A couple of times the paint brush attempted to roll off its purchase, but both times he caught it, adjusted it, and made sure everything was neatly arranged, properly ordered—not an item out of place.

He adjusted the small bottles of acrylic in order of color. The painter felt you could learn a lot by the colors someone liked. In fact, it was often his opener. His current muse had mentioned her favorite color was aquamarine.

Now, she was crying from eyes that weren't *quite* aquamarine, but close enough that most wouldn't see the point in quibbling.

The artist, though, wasn't *most*.

And his version of quibbling was often a far more strenuous type... and painful.

The woman's legs were tied to the wooden chair. Her hands had been released for her to strike the required pose, but now, as she continued to glance fearfully at the door, his patience was waning.

"Eyes forward, if you please!" he snapped.

She looked ahead quickly, pretending as if she hadn't been ogling the door handle like a divorce attorney watching a voluptuous bartender during happy hour. He'd known a good number of divorce attorneys.

His nose wrinkled, and he stood slowly up, dusting his hands and adjusting his apron fastidiously where it protected his clothing beneath.

Appearances mattered.

Beauty, for beauty's own sake, was a reward in and of itself.

He approached the woman in the chair and watched as she recoiled, exhaling faintly, her breath coming in rapid gasps.

"P-please," she said urgently. "My... my roommates are going to wonder where I am!"

He shook his head once, brushing her hair from her face, behind an ear, and studying her exquisite features. He chose for a very specific reason, and she'd *more* than satisfied his criteria.

"No," he said softly, almost gently, his voice still calm, quiet. His eyes flicked towards the workbench on the other side of the room. When she'd first spotted the tools there—screws, hammers, nails, pliers, she'd panicked.

But what did she think he was? Some sort of sadist?

He wrinkled his nose again and softly murmured to himself.

"Here I love you and the horizon hides you in vain. I love you still among these cold things." He smiled softly at the cadence of the words, the knuckle on his pointer finger grazing her cheek. He said, quietly, "Do you know who penned those words?"

The woman was shaking her head again, sobbing. She was a Freshman at the local college.

Well... *local* where he'd taken her. They'd traveled some hundred miles since. But when he'd recruited her for this project, her vibrancy, her youth, her fresh skin, her smiling eyes... All of it had spoken to him of the beauty in nature itself. The beauty born from the womb.

"Pablo Neruda," he said simply. "Do you know who that is?"

The young woman loosed a small sob, shaking her head feverishly. Her curled hair swished, her hands gripping the edges of her seat. "Please!" she begged, her feet shifting, her skinny jeans rubbing against each other. Her shoes, some newfangled brand beginning to be advertised on the internet. He'd never much understood the appeal of internet, but more and more homes across the United States were slowly opening their doors to the thing.

In fact, he'd heard tell that some companies were attempting to put internet on cellular phones! This young woman had possessed one such phone. He glanced again towards the workbench where the brick-looking device rested next to her purse.

Just a trend, he thought. The car phone, in his opinion, had already been a step too far.

All of this technology, this... this *internet*... was slowly, over time, spoiling creativity. Robbing the mind of those beautiful and deeply necessary silent moments.

"Chin up, please!" he repeated like a doting mother admonishing a child. Again, his fingers trailed against her cheek, this time dropping lower, grabbing her chin and tilting it.

She didn't resist. Just looked at him, those eyes so very wide. Nostrils flared. Sweat just prickling across her forehead and plastering a few of those errant, dark curls against her flawless skin.

"Perfect!" he exclaimed in delight. "Don't move... not an inch, please."

The young woman was hyperventilating, and again her eyes darted to the door.

He shook his head, clicking his tongue, but then turned his back to her, approaching his easel once more. The canvas called to him. As he walked away, he muttered, "*The piers sadden when the afternoon moors there. My life grows tired, hungry to no purpose.* Do you know who that was?"

Then came the sound of a crash. Of splintering.

He turned, raising an eyebrow speculatively as the young woman had thrown herself sideways. She was gasping heavily, crying and screaming.

He just watched, curious. She managed to disentangle herself with the frantic movements of a woman possessed, flinging small shards of wood, scattering them across the ground as she dragged her leg away. She slipped a couple of times on the debris she'd caused and let out a strangled, little moan of terror before releasing another desperate, incoherent scream.

He didn't move, preferring to simply watch speculatively.

Then, as she managed to rise to her feet again, having shaken free one splintered leg of the wooden chair, he reached for his paintbrush again, humming softly to himself. A concerto of his own devising. He wasn't *just* a painter. How predictable.

He shook his head but refused to roll his eyes—an uncouth gesture.

He delicately adjusted the strings on his apron, tightening it, then leaned into his painting, adding a few more touches.

It was a strange juxtaposition of moments. The painter standing there, humming softly, brushing reds against the canvas. Meanwhile, the terrified woman was screaming, dragging a mangled chair—which was still roped to her right leg—towards the door. She grabbed the door handle, breathing heavily.

Twisted.

Locked.

She tried to pull more desperately. Still locked. A metal door, only opened with a key. A key in his pocket.

He glanced up, amused, then glanced back down again, focusing on this next, tricky part. His tongue tucked inside his cheek and he pulled the paintbrush in a semi-circle across the canvas. Red for anger. Red for fear. He added a bit more of the hue, then turned to orange.

"Yes..." he said. "There we are."

The woman, shooting a panicked look towards him, released another desperate scream then spun on her heel and tried to sprint away from him.

The small, windowless room had an adjoining hall. She hastened past the workbench with her fancy, new, mobile phone and her purse, ignoring the items—or perhaps not noticing them in her haste.

She then reached the opposite room, where he sometimes slept when the inspiration hadn't struck him.

"There are no doors there! Please don't dishevel the bed—it irks me so!" he called out, absentmindedly. Then he returned his attention to the easel once more. He leaned back on one heel, crossing one arm over his chest, the other extended away from his body, still gripping the paintbrush, which he tapped a few times against his thumb. A few flecks of color spattered the newspaper he'd carefully laid on the ground.

He had *other* leaves of newsprint and plastic sheeting set on the workbench too. But *that* was for a different mess that he wouldn't clean up until later.

Granted, if she kept hollering like this, he might expedite that particular portion of the artistry.

Most of his masterpieces required a finishing touch. The muses themselves included in the artwork.

He watched as the woman returned down the hall, pale, breathing desperately and gripping a splintered chair leg like a cudgel in one hand.

He ignored her.

She charged at him.

He hesitated, added another small stroke of the paintbrush.

SHE RUNS AWAY

And then she was on him.

Only then did he move *fast*.

Very fast.

What they saw: painter. Social elite. Aristocrat. At least, these were the labels he might have merrily accepted.

What they didn't see?

Three tours overseas. Special forces for two of them. Sniper school. Demolitions. And hand-to-hand combat training with Mossad *and* fringe members of Dagestani martial artists.

And it was this *second* type of artistry that took over as she swung the splintered, makeshift cudgel at his head. He ducked, caught her arm on his forearm, sent his open hand into her throat and she reeled back, gasping and gagging.

To her credit, the fight didn't leave.

One good throat punch often knocked the zeal right out of amateurs.

But the young woman, gasping, tried to attack him again. He hit her once more. This time almost lazily, like an alpha lion batting a cub away with a paw.

His heart wasn't in it—he just didn't want her ruining his work.

Now gasping, struck twice and dazed, she stumbled away. Blinking... she stared at him, mouth unhinged. She let out a faint gasp. "Wh-who are you?" she whimpered.

He ignored her once more.

"Please, sit down," he said quietly.

She was unbound. Hands free. Her weapon had been taken from her, and he held it firmly. He glanced towards her then extended her makeshift cudgel back to her. "Please put that with the rest. I'll tend to it later, my dear. Ah, here we go. That's what we need..." He trailed off, returning his full attention to his easel once more.

The painting was *really* shaping up. "The last one auctioned for three million, did you know that?" he said, smiling and allowing the vice of pride a brief abatement in his words.

The woman just stared at him, aghast. She glanced at the wooden club he'd simply handed back to her; half lifted it, breathing heavily, nostrils like a race horse's widening and closing with each desperate inhale.

He raised an eyebrow at her. Didn't raise a hand. Didn't threaten, just quirked a brow. "Sit down, please," he murmured.

She hesitated; stared at him. Then the small wooden cudgel fell from her fingers.

She turned on her heel, glancing back towards her phone on the workbench. As if reading her mind, he said, "The battery is out, dear. Now please, sit down. We're almost done. I'd ask you not to be scared... but honestly, your fear is an expected *and* appropriate reaction. So feel as much fear as you like. In fact, I'm quite enjoying the addition to this piece. Maybe I'll call it... *Fear of Fate!*" He spread his fingers in front of him as if framing some billboard.

The young woman just stumbled back, stepping amidst splintered wood, letting out a faint wheeze. And then she collapsed, slowly stumbling. Leaning back against the wall and sliding down to the floor.

"Go on," he said quietly. "Sit."

She finally did, tucking her legs under her, her hands—trembling horribly—resting on her knees.

SHE RUNS AWAY

She couldn't run. No windows, door locked. Couldn't fight him. Her phone was useless without a battery. Her eyes darted towards some of the hefty tools on the workbench.

He shook his head, again realizing the direction of her thoughts.

He was no mind-reader, but after so *very many* projects just like this one, he'd become somewhat acclimated to the choices his muses made. Threaten, beg, offer favors, plead, fight, run, bleed... It was all the same.

But they didn't have anything he wanted. Once upon a time, years ago, he'd found himself briefly aroused by the offers of one of his muses.

And so he'd personally made sure he was *never* aroused again. Like the old philosopher, Origen. A eunuch by his own hand.

And now he was *truly* free from the bondage of desire.

All that remained was imagination, creativity.

The beauty of it.

The muses had no claim over him.

And that was exactly how he liked it.

But as the trembling young woman glanced towards the workbench again, he said softly, "Whatever you pick up, I will use on you. Are we clear? I don't mean to be harsh, dear, but this is a bit time sensitive, and you're starting to irritate me."

Her eyes widened briefly, and she tore her gaze away from where she'd been eyeing the hammer.

She just let out a wheezing deflated breath. He could see the acceptance settling. The knowledge that *nothing* she did would improve her situation. And finally, with a small moan, she slumped in on herself.

No fighting. No escape. No screaming.

She'd tried it all and it hadn't worked.

"Just look beautiful... and frightened," he said simply. "That's all I need from you..." He sighed. "Sometimes, dear, I even lie to the muses. I tell them things like I'll let them go if they behave. Or I won't hurt them. But you? You don't need the lies." He smiled, looking over his paintbrush for a moment and then giving a faint, delighted whistle. "You really are perfect, though. No... No, my heart couldn't bear lying to a beauty like you. I am going to hurt you. And I'm not going to let you go. But just enjoy it while it lasts, alright? I'm going to make you famous."

She didn't reply.

At this point, they never did.

He began humming again, adding the finishing touches on the painting. The final part—the sealing embellishment—unique to his own masterpieces, would come in a bit.

She didn't need to know about that.

Not yet.

CHAPTER 1

Twenty years later...

She'd never thought she might stoop this low... to do something like her *father* might. But now, on the run with a rogue FBI agent, Artemis Blythe found herself faking a séance in order to save a life.

Her mismatched eyes—one the color of moonlit frost, the other of burnished-gold—flashed in the darkened room. A low wreath of smoke filled the room, and Artemis tried not to blink. Her nose itched, but she didn't want to sneeze either. Any misstep and the entire spectacle would be ruined.

But she made a mental note, glancing at the sputtering flames spread on the table around her, to *never* use the cheap brand of incense candles again. She kept her hands on the wooden table, leaning back in the chair, which creaked from the motion.

She stared as if off into the distance, her eyes narrowed in the smoke-infused room.

A faint gust of cold wind wafted through the room, lingering on her skin and causing prickles to rise on her neck, her arms.

She shivered faintly at the scent of lakewater on the air.

Back in Pinelake once again. Her hometown. And yet her mind wasn't settled. In part, home had never been where her heart was.

But also... a piece of heart was currently missing. Like a jigsaw puzzle with a single gap in the center.

Currently, she was searching under the table, the carpet, combing the floor in search of the missing piece. But her metaphorical search did little to remove the absolute sense of dread lingering in her mind, in her chest like a clot.

She inhaled faintly, the scent of incense itching at her nose. Her fingers clenched and unclenched on the table. She shot a quick look towards the pale-haired woman across the table.

Tears streaked the woman's face where she sat in the comfy recliner. Though the cushioned seat was meant for ease, the woman sat upright, leaning forward, attentive to every detail of the strange ceremony.

"I think I feel something," Artemis said with a small, dramatic exhale.

The woman across the table gasped, hands slapping the wooden surface with a faint *clap*. She watched wide-eyed. "What do you see?" the woman demanded. "Is it her? Is it... is it *him*..." she said, her volume increasing.

Artemis closed her eyes briefly. Another dramatic pause.

But also, she simply needed a moment to allow her conscience to recover. She didn't wince, but she wanted to. In any other situation, given any other set of circumstances, she never would've gone through with the fake séance.

SHE RUNS AWAY

Unlike Cameron Forester, Artemis Blythe did *not* believe in psychics. She'd seen too much farce, growing up, to believe the real thing might exist.

And yet, it was to her shame that Artemis was using more than one of the tactics her father had taught her in order to ensnare the attention of a willing audience.

The room with the boarded windows blocking out the light. The single open window only allowing a beam of sunlight to cut through the faint mist of smoke. The smoke itself, the scent of the candles, the haunting flicker of the flames...

All of it designed to dramatize. To create an aura. All of it completely useless.

Artemis wasn't a mind-reader. She couldn't commune with the dead.

Sometimes, it felt as if she couldn't really commune with the living either. Artemis' lips pressed into a thin line, and her pale brow furrowed as she brushed her coal-black hair behind an ear with a deft, practiced movement.

Normally, she kept her hair in a simple ponytail, to attract as little attention as possible.

But now, her hair was curled if only to add to the aura of mystique and beauty. Even the clothing she now wore had been bought new. From a department store, no less. Most of her clothing she purchased online, a couple of sizes too big. She liked baggy sweaters and sweatpants—though some called her pretty, she didn't like accentuating her appearance. No makeup. The scent of soap instead of perfume...

At least...

Normally, that's how she would've dressed.

Now, she wore an expensive red dress—the tag still attached so she could return it—with a revealing slit up the thigh. Her hair curled, smelling of some strange, luxury-brand shampoo. The perfume she wore also mingled heavily with the odor from the candles.

She was even wearing makeup.

All of it designed to impress.

To make a specific impression on a specific client.

The woman across from her was also dressed nicely. A simple, black dress. The color of mourning. The woman had been mourning for nearly twenty years now.

Artemis had gone over *all* of the news articles they had found. All of the private posts online they'd managed to access with Forester's connections. For nearly three days now, Artemis had been living a life on the run.

Wanted by the FBI for the murder of one of their own.

Wanted by the local police for breaking and entering into one of the deputies' homes, and also for the murder of a fellow chess master.

Artemis Blythe: wanted.

It had a ring to it.

Not a *nice* ring, but a ring all the same.

"I... I think I see something," Artemis began, wincing and exhaling faintly, allowing the smoke to waft past her face. "Yes... Yes, I think I do. A smile... Hmm... Blonde hair. A yellow vest..."

"That's her roommate!" exclaimed the older woman in the black dress. Her hair was cut very close to her head—almost shaved. She had dark skin and perfectly-applied lipstick that made her lips take on the color of berries.

Artemis nodded... "Her roommate... yes..." She hesitated, closing her eyes and even raising a hand to press two fingers against the side of her temple. Instantly, she felt embarrassed by the embellishment and dropped her hand.

Forester was watching over the camera from the other room, after all. And he was occasionally squawking in her ear. *Helping,* he called it. *Annoying,* she called it.

"The roommate's name... I'm seeing an S... S... something..." Artemis paused. "Samantha?"

The old woman across the table gasped, still sitting straight-backed in that recliner, her eyes now widening to the size of saucers. She gaped a second, mouth opening and closing like some fish. At last, she let out a faint sigh. "Yes! Yes, just that! I remember Samantha. A wretched, fat, little girl. Far, far below my Bella's status. But... Bella always had a soft spot for the strays of the world." Mrs. Doler sniffed now, and her features creased into a deep frown. The tears were still trailing along her cheeks, but she reached up a long, perfectly manicured fingernail, wiping away a tear.

Artemis didn't reply at first, waiting a moment. She cycled through her memory, flitting from one article to the next. Every case file from twenty years ago had already been committed to memory. Every newspaper post that had been eventually uploaded to some online database.

And there were a good number of people who still tracked the case of the Aristocrat.

A murderer among the social elite. A killer, who fancied himself something of a painter and poet, who had targeted eight young women over the course of a decade.

And then he'd stopped.

For twenty years, the Aristocrat had gone silent.

"They never found him..." Artemis whispered. "Did they? The police never even had a suspect. They said they did... but they were lying. They never knew who did this to your daughter. They were completely baffled."

The older woman gave a gasp and nodded hurriedly. "I long suspected just this! They didn't know! I don't think they *ever* knew! Liars, the lot of them! They never found my Bella! Never! Do... do you think she's still out there? Is that how you know all of this?"

"No!" Artemis said sharply. She frowned, her brow furrowing. Quickly, she returned her expression to an impassive one.

All of this bothered her.

She didn't like misleading Mrs. Doler. Didn't like making a mockery of her own skills as a thinker and strategist, playing at psychic—the way her own father had often played.

She felt faint tremors as she considered her father. And a foul taste lingered in her mouth. The anxiety in her chest continued to mount.

For a brief moment, Artemis felt a flash of extreme guilt. She'd been attempting to suppress the emotion.

She was playing on a woman's emotions. Playing on this middle-aged woman, still wearing black as if in a constant cycle of grief. She was lying to Mrs. Doler's face. Lying about everything.

And why?

Well... for a *very* good reason. That was why.

But she couldn't continue with it, could she? She didn't want to press further. Already, Artemis felt like she'd crossed boundaries that could never be uncrossed. She was a charlatan. A farce. Pretending to be something she wasn't.

At least she'd refused to take Mrs. Doler's money.

There was that.

A small but somewhat meaningful solace in it all. Her father had done it for money. Artemis refused to.

She was doing it to save a life.

Two lives.

Her mind flashed back to that horrible night on the ranch. The Washingtons unconscious, drugged on the floor. The balloons leaking and descending from the ceiling, hovering halfway up the air, levitating eerily. The phone ringing on the wall.

Answering the phone.

And then the voice...

The woman who'd been haunting Artemis. The woman who'd *lied* about being Helen; who'd *pretended* to be Artemis' sister for some unknown and malicious reason.

A reason that had culminated in a demand.

Either Artemis had to set her father free—breaking him out of jail. *Or* Fake Helen would kill Jamie and Sophie. Jamie... Artemis' childhood sweetheart. The two of them had grown close again, especially after tragedy had struck Jamie's family as well. His mother, killed by his father. His father, killed by the FBI.

Sophie was Jamie's younger sister. He doted on the girl, giving her everything he could think to. He'd even bought the ranch in part so she could have some horses. Sophie had always loved animals.

But now...

The ranch was a crime scene. An FBI agent had been killed on the ranch. And everyone blamed Artemis.

"Just a bit more," the voice said in her ear. She winced, shifting uncomfortably and pretending to adjust a dangling clip-on earring—her ears weren't pierced—while fiddling with the hidden earbud Forester had provided her.

"I'm... thinking..." Artemis said out loud, scowling at the table and the back of her hands.

"Yeah... I can see that, Checkers. We need to go. Can't stay in one place this long." Forester's usual lazy drawl had an edge to it now.

All of this had been his idea.

At least... at first.

But Artemis had taken the idea and *ran* with it. And now...

Now she was in a fake psychic studio built into a small rental unit they'd borrowed from Tommy—Artemis' brother with connections to the Seattle mob. The scent of her perfume, of the incense, was beginning to give her a headache, but she pushed through...

Too much was counting on this.

The voice in her ear said, *"Ask her about her husband."*

"No!" Artemis said quickly.

"Excuse me?" Mrs. Doler said, still sniffling and wiping at her eyes.

"Umm, sorry. Not you," Artemis replied.

"Nice going."

"Be quiet!" Artemis winced suddenly and waved a hand through the smoke, causing it to swirl in undulating patterns. "Sorry," she said to Mrs. Doler, who was now staring at Artemis with a look of surprise and fear. "Just, sometimes, the spirits can talk too much," Artemis said. "It's very distracting. *Very*," she said a bit more emphatically, tapping a finger against the earbud and hoping Forester got the message.

"Besides," Artemis said. "It's far too *early* to ask about that particular thing."

"I... I'm sorry. Ask about what, Ms. Kruger?"

Artemis resisted the urge to roll her eyes. Francis Kruger. The name Forester had given her when setting up this whole ruse. Her fake husband was named Freddy.

Artemis hesitated then said, "You know... I think I'm getting more. Bella was only nineteen when she disappeared. Isn't that right?"

"Yes!" the woman said. But she was leaning back now, resting her head against the cushioned seat at her back. She was also watching Artemis with a curious expression.

Something bordering suspicion, perhaps?

Artemis was playing with fire. The sooner she went fishing for what they needed, the sooner she could get out of here.

Her earpiece was buzzing now, suggesting Forester had accidentally left his feed on. She itched at her ear, and tried, "There were a few other girls, weren't there? Eight?"

"Mhmm... Say, are you from around here, Mrs. Kruger?"

"Umm... No. No, just recently arrived. As you can tell, the place is somewhat new."

"Yes... I saw your ad in the mail. I looked you up online—everyone says you're the best they've ever visited."

Artemis nodded slowly. Inwardly, her sense of guilt only increased. Forester had set the website up. The fake reviews too. On top of that, Forester had been the one to *deliver* the piece of mail. Twice. The first time, it had been thrown out. Likely because *Mr.* Doler had been the one to initially find it.

If they'd been able to access Mr. Doler to start, it would've made things much, much easier.

But it was his *wife* who, according to her credit card statements, spent an inordinate amount on psychics, mediums and the like.

And so Mrs. Doler was their way *in*.

Her husband, on the other hand, was the *real* target.

The warden of the prison where Artemis' father was currently being kept.

"*Gotta hurry,*" Forester said. "*Your brother just texted me. Says a couple of drug dealers were gonna use this place to lay low for a day or two. They're en route as we speak.*"

Artemis' hands clenched tightly, but she slowly unwound them. Her heart was still pounding, fit to burst, but Artemis said. "Mrs. Doler, I was wondering if—"

"No, wait. Let me say something." Mrs. Doler was leaning back again. And now, her eyes were narrowed and held a distinctly suspicious quality to them. She said, "I've dealt with fakes before, you know. When I read your reviews online, I was concerned it might be too good to be true. So I had one of my contacts," she said this word with a self-important tilt of her eyebrows, "do some digging, Mrs. Kruger. Your name... it doesn't show up *anywhere*. And your husband's name... Freddy Kruger?"

Artemis winced, inwardly cursing Forester's bleak sense of humor a million different ways.

But instead of pointing out that the name Freddy K belonged to a fictional serial killer, Mrs. Doler said, "Also doesn't show up anywhere. I understand a need for privacy... Especially with your..." she sniffed, waved a manicured hand in a flourish, "particular gift. But please...

I've been to all sorts who claim to have a connection with the other side. I know how it must look to you. The only reason I agreed to this sit-down was because you refused my money. That and... I had hoped you might tell me something I didn't already know."

The woman sniffed, wiping her face clear of tears now. The emotion from the earlier displays had vanished. Mrs. Doler had calmed, and her pale, close-cropped hair caught the firelight in interesting patterns. This was a woman seasoned with experience. Who *knew* what it was to be taken in by a fake.

This was a woman who'd been searching for hope.

The body of her daughter had never been found.

Another connection point.

Artemis' own sister, Helen, had disappeared almost two decades ago. And *her* body had never been found either.

Artemis knew what it was to retain hope... hanging on to even the *smallest* thread. Artemis also knew history. She read—it helped expand her mind. Helped her prepare for particularly challenging chess tournaments.

But Artemis had read once that Abraham Lincoln's wife, following the death of her own children, had often spent money and time communing with the dead. Or attempting to.

To leave a wound unhealed... to keep opening it rather than allowing a scar to form... some called it hope. Others called it masochism.

Artemis still wasn't sure which one she participated in.

But she was beginning to fear that taking advantage of Mrs. Doler like this was going to yield only more pain.

And so Artemis held up a finger. "Apologies. I understand your skepticism. After so many decades, I have to imagine... things have been difficult."

Mrs. Doler's eyes flashed. Her handsome features arranged into an imperious glare. "You have no idea," she said simply. "If you *really* are hearing... *Seeing*. Then tell me something new. Something I don't already know... Well?"

Artemis let out a small breath.

She closed her eyes briefly, scanning through the memorized portions of the case files, the newspaper articles. All the things that Mrs. Doler herself must've had access too, or attempted to access at the very least.

The items of information that might've come out in interviews or in follow-up questioning.

No... none of that would do.

Artemis leaned back now as well, steepling her fingers and steeling her own spine.

She needed access to Mr. Doler, the warden at her father's prison. She needed access in order to help her own father—the man she hated most—to escape. Her father had been a killer too.

But the woman on the phone, the psychotic woman who'd kidnapped Jamie and Sophie had given an ultimatum.

If Artemis didn't break her own father out of prison *within the week,* then she was going to kill the man Artemis loved. Going to kill Jamie's little sister. A few days had already passed, and it felt as if they were spinning their wheels.

"*Don't think about it. Just ask. Press!*" Forester's voice buzzed over the earpiece.

It was easy for him to say. Forester wasn't exactly what one might call *normal*. He was a self-confessed sociopath. Essentially, he had a very limited conscience. If any at all. His conscience certainly didn't function in the way most humans' did.

The idea of taking advantage of a woman in grief didn't bother him. And yet...

It was the only way she'd been able to think of. The only weakness they'd found, after sleepless nights of searching. Trying to find some way into that prison. Some weakness. Some access point.

The warden's wife.

And so they sat here, facing each other.

The least Artemis could do, she decided—her insides still worming with guilt—was to give the woman hope. Not from a news article. Not from some case files...

But from *truth*. Mrs. Doler deserved that much, didn't she?

The truth.

At least a piece of it?

The sort of truth Artemis was uniquely equipped to offer.

And so Artemis sighed, opened her eyes, and then, her voice low and soft, she began to speak. And Mrs. Doler leaned in to listen.

CHAPTER 2

"I can tell you..." Artemis said quietly, "That you loved Bella more than you loved Tiffany, your eldest daughter... And I can tell you it's because Bella kept a secret for you... Didn't she? Infidelity?" Artemis allowed the words to linger, letting the incense, the lingering smoke, the candlelight, work their magic.

Now, Mrs. Doler had gone still. She leaned forward ever so slightly, her perfectly manicured fingernails tap-tap-tapping against the table.

She stared at Artemis. And some of the scorn and suspicion had vanished.

Artemis, meanwhile, attempted to look omniscient and wise. Really, she felt silly and embarrassed.

Guesswork. Guesswork and human empathy. Artemis had been brought up by a mentalist who'd played at psychic. Her father had run a successful show in the area for years, offering people hope and awe in exchange for their money.

Along the way, Artemis had picked up a few things.

The notion that Mrs. Doler loved Bella more than her eldest daughter wasn't a far reach. In the family photos found in the newspapers, the father had stood on one side, the mother on the other, and the daughters in between. Always with Tiffany closest to her father and Bella closest to her mother.

The interviews Artemis had read also had Mrs. Doler speaking in superlatives about her missing offspring, while only faintly mentioning her eldest.

An easy enough guess.

Part of the benefit of speaking and *processing* quickly was that most people took a minute or two to jump from one syllogism to the next. To move from A to B to C to D to a conclusion. Artemis' mind zipped through the steps. So in an instant, she went from A to D. B and C were intuited.

It was the mind of a world-class chess player. A mind that had tested well above 140 in Mensa practicums.

But there was more to the intuition than simply a mind.

There was also empathy.

Bella had kept a secret for her mother.

For one, most adult offspring kept secrets for their parents, even if something small. But secondly, and more importantly, Artemis had often detected a note of *guilt* in Mrs. Doler's language surrounding her daughter. It had taken some doing, but over time, Artemis had determined it wasn't because of something Mrs. Doler had contributed to the disappearance but, rather, something *prior*, something that still ate at her.

Artemis didn't know if it involved infidelity.

And the moment she *asked*, she knew she was wrong.

Doler had been leaning forward. The moment Artemis guessed, *infidelity?* The woman leaned back now, frowning faintly.

And so Artemis moved quickly on.

This was the benefit of 50-50 stream of consciousness. To ask so many questions or provide so many directives in a short span of time that the misses were glossed over or forgotten, but the hits were seen as proof of supernatural powers.

"H...how do you know that?" Doler was saying, swallowing.

Artemis didn't blink. She'd been wrong about infidelity. So she tried a second guess. "Money issues, weren't they?"

No reason to guess it. But sex, power, money... the three big ones. Aphrodite, Ares and Mammon.

But again, Doler just frowned, opening her mouth to reply. To correct Artemis. But Artemis did it for her. By correcting *herself*, it allowed Artemis to maintain a veneer of omniscience. And so she quickly said, "No, no, of course not. It had to do with your marriage. Not infidelity. Not money. Something... your husband is a very controlling man, isn't he?"

Bingo. Doler was leaning back with her hands folded defensively now. As if intimidated. Hands clasped over her vulnerable core. Her eyes were wide instead of narrowed now.

"Hey... those drug-dealer friends of your little bro's? Five minutes out, Artemis. We need to vamoose!"

She reached up and tried to pull out the earpiece. But before she could slip it into one hand, Doler was saying. "I... I never told anyone that. Wow... you really are the real deal, aren't you?"

Artemis just smiled. Inwardly her mind was accusing her of all sorts of nasty things. Instead, she said, "Your daughter *truly* loved you."

Doler flinched. "I... *Loved.* Are you saying she's..."

Artemis winced. It wasn't her place to take hope away from this woman. But the victim's blood had been found in the Aristocrat's paintings. The victim had been nineteen at the time of her disappearance. Twenty years later, now, she was still gone.

How was it different from Helen?

A small, horrible part of Artemis realized it wasn't *very* different at all. But another part of her refused to draw the connection. Hope for me, not for thee.

But also... false hope was eating at this woman. False hope was costing this woman a fortune.

Artemis could see *other* things. The manicured fingernails, the close-cut hair, all of it communicated a desire to keep things in order, neat. But the woman's wedding ring sat on her ring finger... A few *other* rings sat on the other fingers.

A small, very small, psychological dilution. Some people wanted their wedding ring to be the main item on display. To scream fidelity. But to add *other* rings, and in some cases, more valuable, expensive rings surrounding it? To Artemis, this communicated an attempt to downplay, to disguise, to camouflage.

Plus, no husband liked his wife disappearing at odd hours. This was partly the reason why Artemis had chosen to meet so early in the morning.

To see if Mrs. Doler had that sort of autonomy.

And she did.

"Your marriage isn't doing well, is it?" Artemis said quietly. A guess, but an educated one. "It has to do with your daughter's disappearance... but not *just* that." A very flimsy, loose guess, but it would hit emotional markers so it would be perceived as acute. Artemis finally said, "Your husband resents the credit card bills. In fact, recently, he has proposed to separate finances, hasn't he?"

Doler was now gaping. Gone was her attempt at cold, distant dignity. Now she was like a schoolgirl, excited, vibrant and wide-eyed. "Yes! Yes, he did!" Just as quickly though, the excitement vanished, as she remembered her earlier question. Eyes narrowed again. Lips pressed tight. She murmured, "So... where's my daughter? You said *loved*. Past tense."

It wasn't Artemis' place. But if she could do a little good in all of this, maybe even help save a marriage... It was like a doctor cleaning out a wound. It would hurt but eventually allow the wound to heal.

It wasn't her place. She knew that. But none of this was right. She was playing on this woman's emotions, and Artemis simply couldn't leave without giving *something* in return. Artemis said, as carefully as she could, "Your daughter would want you to move on with your life. To say goodbye. To grieve."

"But... so you *are* saying..." Doler trailed off, frowning.

No tears. Not gasp. No look of sudden panic and pain. Doler had *known* this. It was written all over her face. Her posture. She'd known her daughter was dead. But couldn't move on until she'd been given *proof*.

Artemis justified it in this way, at least. She was only helping to convince the woman of something she already believed.

Artemis leaned in, eyes closed. She wasn't sure she could look the grief-stricken woman in the eyes.

"Two minutes, Checkers. I will shoot these guys if I have to. Just sayin'."

Artemis spoke quickly, the words erupting past her lips like water released from a dam. "Your daughter died peacefully. There was no pain. She was thinking of you. She still is—still *loves* you very much. But you have too much to do in this life to dwell on death. Your daughter Tiffany... she needs you."

Artemis spoke with authority she didn't have, with confidence she didn't feel.

But now... time was ticking. They needed something from this meeting. Artemis said, finally, "I... oh wow... wow... I think I hear more! Something... Something very powerful."

"What is it?" Doler asked, her voice small and thin.

Artemis looked at the woman. "I'm so very sorry for all of this..."

"No... No, it's important I hear the truth," the woman replied, misinterpreting the apology.

"Artemis!"

"I'm coming," Artemis snapped.

And this time, Doler seemed to simply chalk the comment off to Artemis' burgeoning gift. But finally, Artemis said, "I... I have to go now, Mrs. Doler."

"Wait—what? No! No, you can't go! Please! I'll pay you triple."

"I don't want your money, ma'am."

"What do you want then?" The woman asked, wringing her hands. "Please... Please you have to tell me more!"

Artemis paused, inhaling slowly, then said, "I can meet you again. Tonight."

"Tonight?"

"Yes."

Doler hesitated, letting out a long breath. "I... I suppose I can wait a bit longer. It's been so long. Please, couldn't you just tell me what she's saying? Tell me more!"

"Tonight."

Doler looked sick. Artemis felt sick. But her mind went back to Jamie Kramer and his sister. Artemis didn't let the image of them slip from her mind. The danger they were in.

Hands clammy, cold, brow-slick, Artemis said at last, "But we can't meet here. I'm sorry. I... I feel something wrong. Something bad is about to happen to this place."

"Laying it on thick. I like it. A black SUV just pulled up outside."

Artemis reached up this time, removed the earpiece and slipped it into her pocket, pretending as if she were simply scratching.

Doler didn't notice a thing. "Something bad is... wait. Where do you want to meet?"

Fists were now thumping on the door. Loud banging sounds. Artemis cursed, glancing towards the sealed and locked door. But then ignoring it. Pretending as if she'd expected this all along, rather than having been notified about the possibility of disturbance only a few minutes before.

Doler shot a panicked look at the door.

"Is that another client?"

Artemis paused. "We can't meet here."

"So where then? The library?"

Artemis shook her head.

It was *crucial* Doler came up with the location. For her to think it was her own idea, to alleviate any suspicion. But Artemis didn't have time. And her mark needed some guidance.

The fists continued to pound against the door. Artemis said, quickly, "Is there any place that's private in the evening? Around six?"

She knew the warden's schedule. Mr. Doler worked until eight.

"I... I mean... private? There's..."

"Not the church," Artemis said quickly. "It interferes with my connection."

Doler sighed, closing her eyes for a moment.

"Hey—who the hell is in there!" a voice was shouting now.

Doler kept glancing between the door and Artemis as if not quite sure where to focus her attention. Artemis felt another pang of guilt and reached out, touching the woman's hand in a comforting gesture.

Glancing down at the hand, the woman said simply, "Alright... *alright*! I know. What about my house? My husband is out. He doesn't have to know."

Artemis paused. "Well... I don't *normally* do house calls. Maybe it's best we just leave it—"

"No! No! Please!"

Artemis paused. A long pause. The sounds from outside had suddenly gone quiet now. No more yelling. No more pounding. She winced. Glanced back at Mrs. Doler, then said. "I suppose I can make an exception this once. What's your address—actually... Text it to me, please. We should be going."

Artemis stood to her feet. Leaned in, blowing out the incense candles. Sending a few strands of smoke twirling.

The warden's wife stared at Artemis, longing and suffering in her gaze. In the end, though, she sighed and stood up slowly as well, stepping away from the reclining chair.

The two of them, with Artemis' guidance, moved towards the door while Doler asked a series of follow-up questions. "What does she sound like? Is she okay? Is her spirit doing well? Can I help her?"

Artemis dodged and parried and ignored.

She needed access to Mrs. Doler's home.

Specifically, to her husband, the warden's, computer. And now... though it felt like she'd just sold her soul to do it, Artemis had a date with the warden's private residence at six PM.

One step closer to figuring out how to break her father out of prison.

One step closer to saving Jamie and Sophie's lives.

And yet Artemis just felt dirty... Oily. She wanted to apologize again to Mrs. Doler. But just as much, she wanted a breath of fresh lake air.

She turned the lock on the door and opened it quickly. Mrs. Doler's hand pulled at Artemis' sleeve. "Please," the older woman said. "Please, I need to know something. Before you go. *Please*!"

Artemis glanced back, and she wondered if the warden's wife could see the guilt in her mismatched eyes. But Doler wasn't even looking, instead staring back at the table, towards where the candles were still dripping wax down their cylindrical forms.

Briefly, standing by the door, one hand braced against the handle, Artemis wondered what she expected to find on the other side.

The loud shouting, the thumping knocks had faded. But a part of her didn't worry. Not at all. She had too much experience with Agent Forester to think any different.

Besides...

Her conscience couldn't abide this room much longer.

Chapter 3

Mrs. Doler's hand trailed on Artemis' arm, a light touch but tugging insistently, pleading. "Did she... say anything about..." Doler swallowed hesitantly, glancing side to side. For a brief moment, a look of guilt creased the corners of her eyes once more. But then, Doler released her grip on Artemis' sleeve, loosing a sigh and containing herself. She stood straight-backed once more, sniffed, then said, "Tonight. My place. I'll text you the address. Please..." A swallow. "Please don't be late. We have to finish before my husband gets home."

Artemis met Mrs. Doler's gaze. Let out a little sigh, then said, "Your daughter loved you, Mrs. Doler. Very deeply. You're a good mother. I can tell."

Artemis didn't know if *any* of that was true. But she'd decided to lie in order to save a life. So why not also lie in order to assuage a troubled soul?

She gripped the door handle, twisted and pulled it open, like ripping off a band-aid.

Mrs. Doler gasped faintly.

Artemis just stared grimly at the steps leading up to the door.

A tall man in a half-buttoned suit, with a tattoo visible just past the wrinkled collar along his neck, was smirking towards the two of them. His bedraggled, brownish hair fluttered briefly from the morning breeze.

But it wasn't the man's smirk, nor even his lumpy ear—a gift from his fighting days—which had elicited the gasp from Mrs. Doler.

Rather, it was the three men laying unconscious on the steps at Cameron Forester's feet.

Forester leaned against the rickety wooden rail of the borrowed drug den they'd converted into a psychic studio. He sat nonchalantly, both legs dangling loosely over the rail. "Hey there, ladies," Forester said with a polite nod at each of them. Then, he held up three heavily calloused fingers. "Three," he said simply. "Your brother said two. It was three." He glanced down with chagrin at the unconscious, bruised and bloodied faces of three thin figures wearing baggy clothing.

Artemis noticed that a business card had been tucked inside the greasy waistbands of each of the unconscious drug dealers. Likely the card advertised *BamBam,* the gym in the city Forester co-owned. Back in his days as a professional cage-fighter, Forester had built something of a reputation for himself among the down-and-out types in the city.

Mrs. Doler had frozen stiff. Face pale, hand resting against her chest and occasionally fluttering her fingers like the flapping wings of a wounded bird. "Oh... oh my."

"Don't worry," Forester said, chipper as usual. "I'm a cop." He winked. "Had some rough'uns come by. No biggie. Can I walk you to your car?" He slid off the rail, offering his arm and taking a dainty step over a mean-mugged fellow with a face that looked as if it had recently met a meat tenderizer.

Forester's right hand was also being held gingerly against his side.

Mrs. Doler just gaped at the tall man's extended arm. She shot a quick, panicked look at Artemis.

"He... he's a local cop," she said with a sigh. "I've had some trouble with dealers in the area. Sorry..." Artemis tried to say it all nonchalantly, but she wasn't sure *how* one could say *any* of it without a big heap of mortification.

She was glaring at Forester. He winked at her.

She rolled her eyes.

Mrs. Doler, in a fugue, stepped around the unconscious figures, murmuring, "Oh... oh my." Forester took her arm in a gallant sweeping motion and helped her down the stairs. No sooner had they reached the yellowed yard, though, when Mrs. Doler hastened away, taking quick, hurried steps, her head down as if afraid of being recognized by any potential looky-loos.

This particular street, though, was mostly commercial. A garage across the road, which hadn't opened yet, and a small bike and boat rental near the shore of a lake inlet.

Mrs. Doler hastened to her car, which she'd parked in the garage because of the prominent security camera. Artemis guessed that the woman hadn't noticed the lens was smashed and the camera was disconnected.

By the looks of things, two of her hubcaps were already missing. The expensive vehicle, which Artemis didn't recognize as a matter of pride, started instantly. Headlights flared, brake lights glared, and the vehicle swerved onto the road, hastening away towards greener and safer pastures.

As she left, though, only a few seconds passed before the burner phone Artemis had been using buzzed.

She hesitated, glanced down and spotted an address.

She looked up again.

Forester massaged his knuckles, and his eyes were still twinkling, eternally amused at some unspoken joke. "Well then," Cameron said, the six-foot-four giant shooting her a sidelong look. "That went well."

A figure behind him, whose head rested on one of the wooden stairs, let out a faint groan.

"Oh, you hush," Forester said, frowning back.

Artemis just stared at him.

Forester met her gaze, hesitated, then jammed a thumb over his shoulder at the three unconscious thugs. "I had to."

She didn't say a word.

"I *had* to. One of 'em had a knife."

Artemis shook her head and began moving away from the house.

"Oh come on!" Forester said, easily keeping up with his lanky stride. "They were gonna break down the door! Gonna cause problems. I just gave 'em a quick nap time. Sue me!"

Artemis strode stiffly down the road towards the parking lot of the boat rental kiosk where they'd left their own borrowed vehicle. Another gift from her brother, Tommy, and his mob connections. The car had a fake license plate and a clean record.

For now, that was all Artemis really needed to get around Pinelake undetected.

The clock was ticking, regardless.

"We've only got four days left, Cameron," Artemis said. "We don't have time for shenanigans."

Forester strode alongside her, shrugging as he did. "I mean... should I have just let 'em in or something?"

"No," Artemis muttered crossly.

"Well there ya go. So... how'd it go? We got an in with the warden?"

Artemis stepped over a thin line of barbed wire stretching behind the kiosk, brushing it and causing particles of rust to dislodge. She stood in a patch of weeds and grass, glancing back at Forester, who managed to hop the barbed wire without touching it.

"At her house. Tonight," Artemis said. "Six. Gives us time to see what we can find out about the warden."

Forester tucked his hands into his pockets, nodding slowly. "Good. Very good."

His expression softened somewhat now, studying her carefully. "You did good, Artemis. You did what you had to do."

The two of them had now reached the parked car. Some sort of sports thingy... Ferrardo? Fararino? A very fancy, red thing that looked like a spaceship. Hardly inconspicuous in this town, but it was the only vehicle Tommy had on hand at the time.

At least... that's what her brother had said at the time, but she suspected, somewhat, that giving his twin sister a sports car was his version of humor.

She leaned against the vehicle now, hand resting on the red door frame. The scent of the lakewater lingered on the air, mingling with the odor of rust and refuse from the garage behind them. Most portions of Pinelake were idyllic, like off some postcard.

But *this* particular section of the lake had always been bad news.

She sighed faintly, shaking her head and meeting Forester's gaze. "Yeah, well, I feel like shit. I just lied to a grieving mother for an hour."

Forester shook his head. "Your boyfriend was gonna die if you didn't. Still might. That cute kid too. No time for emotions here, Checkers. Gotta just get the job done."

He moved around the front of the car, a look of glee in his eyes at the prospect of driving the fast car again.

She didn't protest. Letting him drive would give her time to think. The front door opened, but Forester didn't enter, peering over the roof of the car and studying her.

"You did what you had to. And you'll do the same tonight. You just gotta. This'll all be over soon. I promise."

She sighed softly, listening to the faint rustle of the trees around them. She knew he was trying to comfort her, but Artemis had too much on her mind to allow herself *to* be comforted.

Plus... sometimes...

When Forester looked at her like this, concern in his eyes... It was almost like the man was looking at someone else. She'd had this sense from him before. Seven years ago, something tragic had happened to Agent Forester. She still wasn't sure on the details.

Three years ago, according to her own father's hints of information, Cameron had done something... Something illegal.

She didn't know the details of this either.

But she did know that Forester didn't play nice with others. According to Forester's current partner, Agent Desmond Wade, Cameron had already been through *five* other partners.

As a self-confessed sociopath, he was somewhat prickly... but Artemis had been doing some research about sociopaths. She felt a faint frown creasing her features now as she slipped into the passenger side seat, settling in the luxurious, leather-trim seating and listening to the growl of the engine and the chuckles of Cameron, as the car pulled out of the kiosk's lot.

They moved hastily onto one of the lakeside roads.

As they drove, she shot a look towards the scar along Forester's hand which gripped the steering wheel. Sometimes... when he looked at her, he saw someone else.

And from what she'd been reading, sociopaths *weren't* incapable of forming emotional attachments. They *could* sometimes form very strong emotional bonds. But only to one or two people. Oftentimes, a sociopath would connect or attach with an individual.

She remembered the tears in his eyes back at the ranch. The way he'd look at her, concerned and compassionate.

It had scared her nearly as much as anything that night.

The idea, somehow, that her sociopathic partner with the FBI had developed something like... an attachment to her. That he *cared* for her.

It scared her, and she didn't know what to do about it.

One thing at a time, though, she tried to remind herself.

One thing at a time. She shook her head, staring through the windshield, and said, "We need leverage. And we need to figure out how to get you into that house while I'm talking with her."

Forester nodded, hands still gripping the steering wheel. "Still no sound from Dawkins," he said conversationally. "I don't think he recognized me."

Artemis shot him a look now, a genuine note of relief to her voice. "Really? So you're still in the clear?"

"Yeah. For now. My aunt's been blowing up my phone and asking me where I'm at."

"And?"

Forester shrugged. "Told her I was in Texas. Visiting family."

"Do you have family in Texas?"

"Nope."

"Wouldn't... your aunt know that?"

"Yeah, yeah... but it's kinda a thing between us, you know." He shrugged, testing the engine again and creating a blur out of the trees on either side of the dusty road. The speed seemed to relax him a bit. Forester often went at his own pace, marching to the beat of his own drum.

Sometimes that meant he would go below the speed limit. Other times, it meant he would go twice as fast.

"She knows I'm lying," Forester said conversationally. "Which is par for the course. If I started telling the *truth*. That I was still in town and all that. It'd really mess with her."

Artemis frowned, picturing Forester's aunt. Supervising Agent Shauna Grant was the one who'd recruited Artemis as a consultant for the FBI. Agent Grant *tried* to keep her nephew on a short leash... but it hadn't worked so far.

This, Artemis was grateful for, in a way. Without Forester's help, none of this was possible.

"So... if Dawkins didn't see you, and you're in the clear, can you still access the FBI database?"

"Mhmm. Probably best not to let 'em see what I'm checking out, though. My aunt'll be watching like a hawk. *But...*" He looked over. "I did manage to figure out what security system Mr. Doler has."

"Yeah?" Artemis drummed her fingers against her thighs. "Good. Really good. So tonight... at six. We'll be ready?"

"I mean... we're not *kidnapping* the lady, right?" Forester said slowly. "Not that I'm opposed to—"

"No!" Artemis said sharply, staring at him. "No... definitely not." Then, with a grudging mumble, she added, "We just need the warden to *think* we've kidnapped her. There's a difference."

"Feels like a lotta trouble just to—"

"We're not going to kidnap her, Cameron. Just, you do your part. I'll do mine, and we can get over this sordid business as soon as possible."

Even as she said it though, and received no reply from Cameron, Artemis could feel her stomach sinking.

She didn't quite believe her own words.

It was still early in the morning. They had time to prepare. To set everything in motion. They needed leverage on the warden. Needed to use whatever they could to lean on him.

They would only get *one* chance to make their pitch.

And if Mr. Doler rejected their offer...

Artemis would likely spend the rest of her life behind bars.

And the two missing Kramers would be killed.

Chapter 4

Artemis sat on edge in the passenger seat of the sports car, fiddling with her new clip-on earrings. She shifted one leg over the other, feeling both uncomfortable and awkward.

The new dress was even shorter than the first one had been, and now, she found herself continually tugging at the hem, trying to pull it lower to preserve some modicum of decency.

Forester, meanwhile, kept shooting her sidelong glances but pretending as if he wasn't.

She wore her hair up again, curled strands dangling over her eyes until they were brushed away with a flick of her fingers.

Artemis kept adjusting her dress, while simultaneously frowning through the windshield at the large house inside the gated community. "What time is it?" she murmured.

Forester looked at the dash, then glanced back at her. "Five minutes. You good?"

She shook her head. "I feel like a teenager on prom night."

"Huh. Yeah. Well... you ever go to prom?"

Artemis gave him a look, sighed, then returned her attention through the windshield. "No," she murmured. "Was already in the foster system by then. Didn't really see the point."

"Right... early graduation. Seem to remember you mentioning that."

"Mhmm..." she said, hesitating and going back through her mind, replaying memories. She *had* offhand mentioned her earlier graduation to Forester. Weeks ago. Clearly, he'd been listening.

And again, she felt uncomfortable at this thought.

She looked away from the agent who kept watching her out of the corner of his eye. There was something almost... pained about his expression. A grief lingering there. A desire too.

Both emotions, especially from *him,* scared her. She wondered what it might be like to be with a man who *couldn't* be controlled. Forester was like a storm at sea—entirely untameable. She wanted to tell herself she didn't find him attractive, but a small part of herself wondered if she was scared of opening the door to a tempest. She'd always liked being in control. Chess was a way to control pieces in a closed system...

What did that say about Jamie?

She shook her head, frowning. Safe. Kind. Gentle. Handsome. Jamie was... well... *the* Jamie Kramer.

She shook her head, forcing the thoughts from her mind.

"I think we're good," she said simply, smoothing her dress a final time and pushing open the door.

Forester slipped from the front seat as well, and the two of them emerged on either side of the red vehicle, staring towards the house through the gated fence.

"Best entry point is gonna be around the back," Forester said. "There's an electrical grid—closed system—for the gated community. Was set a bit too near the back fence before they extended the boundary. Should be able to up-and-over."

Artemis nodded, breathing carefully. She'd refused high heels. Even the best attempts at making an impression had to be curtailed somewhere.

Now, she fell into step with Forester. He offered his arm in the same way he had with Mrs. Doler while escorting her over three men he'd beaten unconscious. She slipped her arm through his. Not because she wanted to, but because they'd be passing the gate guard, and all of this depended on appearances.

"You got your earpiece in?" Forester said.

"Yes."

"Don't turn it off this time."

"I didn't."

"You did."

"No. I took it out. I didn't turn it off."

"Same difference, Checkers. Come on. You feeling up to this?"

He was watching her now, and this time, instead of the combination of grief and desire she'd spotted earlier, he just looked uncertain.

"I'll be fine," she shot back. "You just have to make sure you disengage the security system. And set up the back patio."

"Yeah... right. Just like we discussed. I'll follow the script, Checkers. Just make sure you do the same. Remember your why, okay?"

"I remember," she said grimly.

SHE RUNS AWAY

The two of them now circled around the path leading through the wooded lot encircling the gated community where Mr. and Mrs. Doler lived.

And, according to Forester, the Pinelake police chief and half a dozen others from the surrounding districts.

As they strolled along the brick path, moving under trees, and along the metal fence encircling the gated community, Artemis kept glancing through the bars at the mansions within, her heart pounding, her stomach twisting horribly.

They had to find leverage on the warden. They'd chosen to use his wife as the vector of attack.

It required a level of heartlessness that Artemis wasn't sure she possessed... no. No, that wasn't true. Far worse... she suspected she *did*.

She'd proven it already, hadn't she?

The two of them now reached the back side of the fence, facing a large, gray square of metal with silver handles on the front wrapped with a chain and padlock.

She eyed the metal breaker box suspiciously. "It won't... electrocute us, will it?"

"Hmm? Nah. Here, you go first."

She glared at him. "No. *You* go first."

"What?"

"You're trying to look up my dress, Cameron. Go."

"I was *not*!" he said, sounding scandalized.

She maintained her glare. "You have a tell when you lie. Now go. Can't say I'll cry if you do get shocked."

Cameron shrugged, hopped up with a quick leap and shove of his arms, and scrambled on top of the large, gray breaker box. He then turned and extended a calloused, scarred hand towards her. The white scar, starting in the center of his palm, climbed up under his forearm, disappearing beneath his sleeve.

She took his hand, carefully, and pushed off the box. Again, she smoothed her dress with her other hand as he lifted her in one quick pull.

It was as if she were as light as a string to the ex-fighter. He wasn't even breathing heavily as he turned and began to clamber up the fence near the breaker box.

Within a few moments, the two of them found themselves hopping off the metal mesh *into* the boundary of the gated community, standing on a perfectly manicured lawn behind a house as large as Jamie Kramer's old home.

The giant house didn't intimidate Artemis the same way similar homes had in the past. She'd learned too much about the sorts of people who lived *within* such buildings to fear them.

More specifically, she'd learned such people were, in fact, *people*. No different than anyone else.

The two of them moved quickly around the side of the large home, hastening forward. Mrs. Doler had provided Artemis' fake name to the gate guard for entry. But an ID would've been required, which Artemis couldn't supply.

So now, with Forester in tow, the two of them hastened towards the Doler residence in the back of the small block.

It wasn't as large as some of the other homes, but it was still a mansion. And through the window of a makeshift turret, Artemis spotted an enormous floor-to-ceiling aquarium.

"Not too late to go back," Artemis said softly.

"Do you want to?" Forester replied.

"No."

"Okay then. I'll meet you in fifteen. Just... be safe."

"Yeah... and Cameron."

"Mhmm..."

She stared at him, her emotions a tangle, her heart in her throat. Adrenaline was racing now, and she felt emboldened. Some of her fear flitted away. She stared at him, nodded once, patted him on the arm and said, "Thank you. Really. You don't have to do any of this. I know that."

He chuckled, ran a hand through his bedraggled hair, then sauntered off, moving around the turret, the blue glow from the aquarium in the dark window illuminating him with a strange aura.

Once he'd disappeared around the back, Artemis turned and hastened towards the front door, where Mrs. Doler was expecting her.

She hurried between two pewter lions set between a row of orange, glowing lanterns. The garden was manicured and boasted perennials. The door itself was mahogany and carried *another* lion sculpture as a knocker.

Artemis' fingers trembled, and she ducked her head in order to avoid the camera over the door. She reached out, swallowed faintly, hand gripping the knocker. Beneath her breath, she muttered, "Hello, Mrs. Doler! A pleasure to see you again..." She frowned, swallowed, tried again. "Hello, Mrs. Doler. What a pleasant surprise."

She sighed, deciding no amount of rehearsal would prepare her for what came next.

Instead, she reached out, gripped the door knocker, and struck the wood twice.

Before the second blow, the front door opened wide. Mrs. Doler stood there, frowning. Her eyes were narrowed again.

And flanking the warden's wife were two large burly men. Muscled and both armed. Guns in hand.

Mrs. Doler glared through the door, staring at Artemis. "Ms. Blythe," Doler said simply.

"I... Excuse me?" Blythe... Artemis' heart leapt. Doler knew her name. Knew who she was. *Shit.* Artemis took a hesitant step back.

"No, my dear," said Mrs. Doler. "Don't. These two young men you see behind me work with my husband. They also do some work for me. They'll make sure you don't leave. Understand? I know who you are Artemis. I didn't earlier today. But like I said, I have contacts of my own."

Artemis was panic-stricken. Could feel her skin prickling with horror. Could feel her heart pounding wildly. She wanted to turn. To run. Wanted to lie.

But Doler's voice was iron. Her eyes icy as she said, "Do come in. Please take off your shoes, my dear. We have a lot to discuss."

CHAPTER 5

Behind Mrs. Doler, Artemis' eyes landed on the wall-to-wall television screens complete with HD images. For a mind-bending moment, Artemis thought she was staring at a mirror.

Her face stared back.

It took her a split-second to realize she was watching the evening news. And all across the screen, her old chess license photograph was being played.

Bold text beneath the images read: *Local Chess Master Commits Murder... Serial Killer's Daughter on the Run!*

Artemis stared, her heart in her throat, her shoulders heavy, as if her entire world were crashing down around her. She opened her mouth, closed it, and stumbled back a second. But then froze as Mrs. Doler clicked her fingers a couple of times, gesturing at Artemis.

"Come on. *Now.*"

No *please,* this time. No *my dear.*

The game was over. Doler *knew* who Artemis was. The fear spiking through her chest was secondary to the trembling in her legs. Suddenly, wearing the dress she'd chosen, attempting to dazzle, to blend, to distract, Artemis felt exposed.

Her legs were cold. Her arms too.

She brushed her curled bangs from her mismatched eyes, staring in horror through the doorway. The two, musclebound men on either side of Mrs. Doler had the look of cops. Off-duty, though, most likely.

"These are my nephews. Glen and Darren. You can introduce yourselves inside. Now *come in*."

Artemis bit her lip and reached a decision.

She wasn't being arrested.

Which meant Doler was handing her rope to hang herself with. But for now... Doler was still the only person who could give them access to the warden at her father's prison. And Artemis had information to work with.

The multiple rings. The secret that the murdered daughter, Bella, had apparently kept. And, most of all, the attention of Mrs. Doler.

Besides, Forester was currently disarming the alarm in the back. The plan, initially, had been to stage a kidnapping while luring Mrs. Doler away. Forester was then supposed to contact the warden and blackmail him. Artemis was going to leave Mrs. Doler in Seattle somewhere, at an exhibit, telling her to wait.

It had been elaborate.

And now, it wasn't going to work.

Artemis didn't turn to run. Didn't see the point. Instead, she pressed her fingers against her palms, not quite bunching them into fists, and stepped forward.

Doler allowed Artemis to enter, side-stepped the younger woman, and shut the door with a loud *thump!*

"You look lovely, my dear," said Doler. "Now please, into the reading room. If you cause any trouble, Glen and Darren are here to help. Darren, make sure she's unarmed."

One of the musclebound nephews, clearly an off-duty cop by his bearing, his haircut and the uncomfortable glance he shot the man named Glen, stepped forward.

He winced, muttering a quick apology.

His hands moved lightly over her, doing his best to maintain decency while simultaneously being thorough under the watch of his aunt.

Artemis just stood stiff, frozen in place. A few seconds later, the man stepped back, holding a little can of pepper spray which Artemis had kept under the two-inch, satin sash that had wrapped around her midsection.

"That's all there is," he said.

Doler glared at the spray, and her eyes darted back up to Artemis. "I see..." the woman said coldly. "Well... After you, Ms. Blythe."

Artemis hesitated, glancing towards the spray. It had been intended as a defensive device only. Just in case.

Now, wishing she'd thought to wear a jacket. Or, hell, *pants,* she moved in the indicated direction. The marble-tiled floor looked as if it had recently been washed. She entered a room with a fireplace in one corner, an ornate, marble mantelpiece and a small, antique clock set on the marble.

Two red chairs faced multiple bookshelves. The books themselves were covered in dust, suggesting the tomes were for appearance's sake rather than perusing.

Mrs. Doler sat in one of the red chairs. Artemis sat across from her, crossing her legs, and folding her hands over her knees.

At the same time, Artemis' eyes darted to a window near one of the bookcases. No sign of Forester.

Shit.

She attempted to remain calm, practicing one of the breathing exercises that her revolving door of shrinks had attempted to impart.

But psychologists, psychiatrists, counselors and everything in between had never been able to quite *fathom* Artemis Blythe. In her younger years, she'd mostly thought this was their fault.

The older she got, though, now passing the first round of thirty, she wondered if maybe it was her fault more than she'd originally considered. It was difficult for others to help when someone refused to be vulnerable.

And if there was one thing Artemis had learned years and years ago. Trusting someone with your heart was a mistake.

At least... *most* someones.

She could think of an exception.

Jamie Kramer's sea-gray eyes set in an olive complexion. His hair neatly parted, his smile warm and kind. In fact, all of him had been warm. She'd often thought of Jamie like a campfire on a cold night. Something about his presence... that made everything okay.

And now he was missing.

And if she didn't hurry, he would die.

But the plan was quickly deteriorating before her eyes.

"You must think me a fool," said Mrs. Doler, hands also clasped, her many rings glinting in the firelight beneath the ornate mantelpiece. The antique clock made a quiet *ticking* sound.

"I don't."

"No, hush. Let me finish. You really must think me a fool. Did you not think I'd look into you?"

Artemis glanced towards the television screens in the main room, then back again.

Mrs. Doler pursed her lips. "I suppose it didn't take very *much* checking, now did it? Artemis Blythe. Two murders. Impressive."

Artemis tensed.

"Normally, my engagement with criminals is limited," Mrs. Doler said softly. Her eyes moved towards the two off-duty cops by the door. Her nephews were watching the exchange not like a couple of dumb thugs waiting for the order to snap a kneecap but with twin expressions of concern and discomfort.

They were here, likely, as a favor. But they also didn't seem comfortable with it. Artemis didn't blame them. They both had intelligent eyes to go with those muscles. Close-cut hair—regulation. Tightly-fitting clothing, like that of some runners. But they were also wearing tennis shoes. And the one named Glen had a faint stain on his shirt. No keys in his pocket. The stain was fresh.

Small details. But details that mattered.

It told her that he'd been eating dinner recently. And hadn't *driven* to get here. But perhaps the other nephew had picked him up…

No. Artemis decided. No jackets. A cool night. They'd walked. Which meant they both lived nearby. Given the demographics in the gated community, she supposed they lived a street or two over.

In addition, Mrs. Doler wouldn't have had very *much* time to get her nephews to come.

Which meant Doler's realization was something of a recent monkey wrench.

All of this information, speculation flashed through Artemis' mind in a split-second. Like the snap of a finger. Unwinding the information, analyzing each piece for a flaw, took longer. But not nearly as long as most minds would've required.

Artemis didn't speak. Didn't mention *any* of this. For now, she just listened, gathering information as quickly as her mind could move.

Doler was saying, "You killed an FBI agent. Someone named... *Butcher*? Is that right? And you also killed a chess player named Azin Kartov. And it has me wondering... Ms. Blythe." Here, Doler leaned forward, her eyes like fragments of a glacier. "How did you know all of that about my Bella's death? Hmm?"

Artemis went still, frozen in place. It took a second, but then the horror washed through her as she realized what Doler was implying.

"I didn't have anything to do with it!" Artemis said firmly, trying to rise from her chair.

But the two men by the door stepped into the room, wearing twin frowns. Their hands had strayed towards their firearms, and Artemis lowered herself again, glancing nervously towards the door, swallowing, then glancing at Doler once more.

The imperious older woman looked as if she'd seen a ghost. Or perhaps simply the daughter of one. Her face was pale, her breaths coming in short, staccato bursts. Shallow breaths, breaths that only touched the lungs before escaping once more. Her chest rose and fell slowly, the ornate, silken shirt with tasseled sleeves following the motion of her breaths of anticipation.

Everything in her body was tense. Her hands tight where they gripped the arm rest of the chair. Her dark features had creased with worry lines.

She didn't blink. Her eyes like silver dollars, like spotlights.

And Artemis couldn't escape the attention.

"Your father..." Doler said quietly. "He's a serial killer, isn't he? He killed your own sister."

"No," Artemis said sharply. She *had* thought this very thing for a long time... but new information had come to light. Helen had appeared to Tommy at a waterfall, years ago. At least... so Tommy said. And he had the letter to prove it.

Doler sneered now. She glanced towards her nephews and waved a hand at Artemis. "See?" the socialite said. "Even now she defends his actions."

Artemis didn't protest. They were on thin ice, and she could hear it cracking. But thankfully, for now, Mrs. Doler didn't mention *anything* about her husband. Perhaps she didn't know, yet, *where* the Ghost Killer, Otto Blythe, was currently being imprisoned.

This woman had a one-track mind. Her focus was on her daughter, and her daughter alone.

Now, she said, "You need to give me a good reason, Artemis, dear, why I shouldn't suspect you're complicit in my own daughter's disappearance. You knew too much. You knew about the secret we had. You knew about my personal life. You said she didn't suffer when she died, and you were so confident that she *was* dead. What am I to think?" The woman said, folding her hands and shaking her head side to side.

Artemis opened her mouth to defend herself, chills erupting down her spine, but before she could speak, the woman gave a quick shake of a single, pointing finger, and said, "I'm not finished yet. This is what's going to happen, you're going to tell me exactly what you did. *How* you were involved."

"I was only ten at the time," Artemis cut in, refusing to let this go any further, and determined to head it off at the pass before it reached critical mass.

Mrs. Doler frowned. "I had considered this. Your father, though. There were rumors that you helped him. A small killer in training."

"That's not what happened at all. I didn't have anything to do with the Aristocrat."

The woman stiffened at the moniker of the man who'd taken her daughter. But Mrs. Doler just sneered, shaking her head. "How did you know all of that? What you told me," she said, hesitantly, her eyes shooting towards her nephews but then darting back towards Artemis in defiance. "Everything you told me back there? Who have you been talking to? Did your father know the killer?"

But Artemis said, insistently, "No. Listen, I'm a private investigator. I work with the FBI."

Mrs. Doler just laughed. A cold, bitter sound. She threw back her head, and her pale, close-cut hair seemed to shimmer and turn silver with the way the shadows caught it as she tilted her chin.

"I'm not lying," Artemis said quickly. "They might've not mentioned that on the news. Probably wouldn't want to associate with me. But I didn't *kill* anyone."

As she said it, she realized just how thin it all sounded. Her protests, likely, were falling on deaf ears.

It all sounded frail. And she knew it.

Her eyes darted to the window again. No sign of Forester. Had he spotted the two off-duty cops? Did he know to stay away?

"Why... why aren't you calling the police?" Artemis said slowly, swallowing once.

Here, Mrs. Doler's eyes flashed. She said, softly, "I hope to do this painlessly, Ms. Blythe. Truly. But I've looked for twenty years for answers. I want to know what happened to my daughter. And you seem to know."

Now, both the nephews were shifting awkwardly, both clearly uncomfortable with the direction of the conversation.

But neither of them protested. Neither of them interjected. If anything, they both carried grim looks of resignation. They knew what their aunt would do, and they'd already decided it was their role to aid her in her endeavors. Whatever that meant.

And it was the *whatever* which currently haunted Artemis' mind. Again, she felt exposed. Vulnerable. She shifted again, her brow warm, her hands trembling. The clot of anxiety in her stomach was growing, tingling along her body.

"I didn't have anything to do with it," Artemis said. "And I don't have any special knowledge. I spotted the rings on your fingers," she said quickly, "And intuited you were diluting the wedding band. I spotted the pictures in newspaper articles, which I read before meeting you, and I intuited the nature of your relationship with your daughter."

"No... No, how would you know I shared a secret with my daughter from that? How did you know she died painlessly?"

"I was guessing. Trying to help!" Artemis exclaimed. "I know what it is to lose someone. My own sister, Helen. How it haunts you. I didn't want to hurt you. I just..."

"Wanted what?" snapped Mrs. Doler. "To taunt me? To come back to the scene of the crime and watch my pain? That's what your type likes to do, don't you?"

"I'm not a killer, ma'am. I'm an investigator and a chess player. That's it. I make connections others don't because I didn't train in an academy. I just... *think* differently."

Artemis could feel her mounting desperation, and again it seemed as if they were heading in some direction from which there was no return. She wasn't sure exactly *where* this direction would take them. But it felt as if Artemis, at least, was going to be shoved off a cliff unless she was abundantly careful.

Now, she could feel herself beginning to hyperventilate. Losing control of regulated breathing.

The panic would set in.

The anxiety would spread.

The last thing she wanted was a panic-attack in the middle of this fire-side library, surrounded by people who were looking at her as if she were something icky found on the bottom of a shoe.

Finally, Artemis said, "What if..." she swallowed. "What if I can give you the answers you need?"

Mrs. Doler smiled. A humorless, thin-lipped expression that didn't so much as *touch* her eyes. "I thought you might."

"Not like that! I didn't have anything to do with it. I only have the information I could glean from the internet and from FBI files."

"I don't believe you *were* part of the FBI," Doler said. "But if you need to maintain this farce for your sake, go ahead. Just so long as you tell me about Bella."

Artemis said, "I can't do that. Not yet. But I can find out."

Her mind was racing a million miles a minute, and she wanted to slow it down. Tried to breathe. The anxiety nearly unbearable. But she knew she was in a tough situation. Knew there was very little opportunity of getting out of this without some sort of pain.

But she also refused to forget Jamie Kramer. Only three and a half more days. That's how long she had to spring her father out of prison. To release an actual serial killer on the world.

She still didn't know how she was going to play it.

She couldn't *actually* let Otto Blythe escape. But the only way to get Jamie and Sophie back was to play along until she could find a way out of this terrible mess.

It was all beginning to be too much.

Her mind kept spinning. Her breath kept coming in puffs. She twisted her hands on the edges of the seat, and her feet scraped the ground as if attempting to carve small rivulets in the slick, gleaming hardwood floor.

Her mind was scattering, and she was struggling to keep it all together.

But something like a plan was forming. A contingency. One of the benefits of preparing for tournaments had been the need to memorize openings. Artemis had particularly enjoyed anything involving a Queen's Gambit. She'd also been fond of the Sicilian.

But openings only went so far.

If the opponent countered with something unconventional, then inevitably, Artemis was forced to improvise. To come up with some *other* tactic.

And currently, it felt as if she was being forced to improvise.

She'd prepared for the match. Had shown up. Started moving pieces.

And then Mrs. Doler had come along and moved an H-file pawn. All Artemis could do was react.

CHAPTER 6

"I'll solve the case," Artemis said finally, the words blurted from her lips. "I will. I'll find out who the Aristocrat is. I'll find out exactly what happened to your daughter."

Mrs. Doler scoffed. "I think you already know."

"I don't. Like I said, I'm intuitive."

"No one's *that* clever. You knew things, Artemis. Things only the killer or an accomplice would know."

Artemis huffed, exhaled, and began glancing around the room. Suddenly, she pointed at Glen. "I know he lives in the same gated community as you. I know he's an off-duty cop."

Glen tensed, staring at her.

Then, for good measure, Artemis added, "Also, his name's not really Glen, is it?"

Now, the man who'd been called Glen looked briefly frightened. His large knuckles tensing against each other.

"See?" Artemis said, turning to Mrs. Doler. "I guessed. And he reacted. But I stated the guess with complete confidence, so it *felt* like knowledge. I didn't know. But now I do. Because *he* told me. Not just him, you as well." Artemis wasn't done. She felt as if she were now performing. Like her father used to. But far more was at stake than money. She gestured towards the second off-duty cop. "Also, his name isn't Darren. No? But D? Yes. See? Again, the eyes. The hesitation. You're keeping your face completely impassive, what some call a poker face. But it's a mistake. A poker face is only useful if it's your *normal* mode of being. But before I started speaking to you, not-Darren, you were twitchy. Blinking every ten seconds. I'm guessing you're wearing contacts, yes? Which means even though you're not wearing a wedding ring, I know you're married. But separated."

Now, a strange silence fell over the room.

"How could you *possibly* know that?" said Mrs. Doler, voice cold.

"The same way I know that his name starts with a D. He reacted in familiarity. And I can guess, though it's just a guess, that there is no letter O after the D. Because his last name, like yours, most likely, would be Doler. And the syllable Do with Doler following would make any self-conscious parent embarrassed. No... so probably a softer sound. Da? Di? I don't know too many Di names. And now, he just reacted at Da. Which narrows it down. I can only think of a few Da names that come instantly to mind. And again, see? He's poker-facing. David. Is your name David? Not Darren, since we established that. But David—Davey?"

The man who'd called himself Darren was looking frightened now. Licking his lips faintly and muttering, "What the hell..."

"See?" Artemis said insistently, her eyes holding a challenge as she turned back to acknowledge the matriarch. "Not to mention," she continued, "I know he's separated for a similar line of reasoning. No wedding ring, right? Who takes off their wedding ring in the evening when they're home with their wife? The contacts, though, suggest to me someone who's concerned with appearance on at least *some* level. He also lives nearby, which means he would've had the time to put contacts in if he'd wanted. But I don't think he did. Why would he? To come hold some strange woman prisoner in his aunt's house? No... No, he's also blinking too much. Which means the contacts have dried out his eyes over time. So he was wearing them at work as well. Making an impression on some coworker perhaps? No... No, not a coworker." Artemis was rattling all this off at the speed of sound. She said, "And see, there? I missed it. But I changed the intonation of the question *halfway* through. I started confident, read the reactions and ended by intonating a question. Softening my commitment to the claim and maintaining my credibility in your eyes. It's all a game. It happens instantly. It's a trick. That's it. A simple trick. I grew up watching my father do it for a living. And as for my father—I hate him. I never helped him, and you may very well not trust me, but I refuse to play along with the claim that I wanted *anything* to do with Otto."

She finished with a faint, huffing breath, her chest rising and falling, her hands clenched at her side.

Everyone was staring at her now. Tense.

A slow, lingering silence filled the room. The flicker of flames from the fireplace illuminated the figures, casting shadows in strange arrays across the slick floor.

No one spoke for a moment.

And then, Mrs. Doler said, carefully... "You really are some sort of genius. That's what they're saying on the television."

Artemis shrugged. "The tests say so. Yes." Never one to scorn an opportunity, Artemis pressed, "Which is *why* I can help find the Aristocrat. Serial killers are often above-average intelligence. Smart people can get arrogant. They think their brief bump in processing speed makes them special. It's pathetic, really. But a reliable assumption."

They were all staring at one another. Artemis just glared back. At last, she said, "The Aristocrat was active twenty years ago. Do you really believe that, as a ten-year-old girl, I was going around helping this serial killer? While *also* helping my father. And it just so happened that *no one* suspected a thing? No one found out?"

"It's possible," Doler said coldly.

Artemis shrugged, leaning back and folding her hands in her lap. She did this in part to give an air of finality but also to disguise the trembling. "In that case," she said simply, "Believe what you wish. I've said what I can. You have to decide what's more important."

Mrs. Doler paused, studying Artemis. Then, quietly, she said, "Why?"

"Excuse me?"

"Why all of this? Why trick me? Why drag me down to that drug den, pretending to be something you're not. You didn't want money... so *why*?"

Artemis hesitated, considering the wisdom of revealing the truth.

But she was pivoting. Improvising. The opening had collapsed, and they were no longer in positions known to most chess databases.

The human element of strategy was often overlooked when preparing for matches. Artemis had never considered herself the most tactical player. She didn't have the most standard lines memorized. In reality, her strength came from reading *people*. In the flaws that were presented.

In a game against a computer, Artemis would likely do the worst out of any of her peers in the chess world.

But tournaments weren't played against computers. It was her knowledge of people that gave her the edge.

And so, at last, Artemis said, quietly, "I'll tell you, if they leave." She nodded towards the men in the door.

"I don't think you're in a negotiating position," said Mrs. Doler softly. "You will tell me *now.*"

But Artemis shook her head simply. "No... No, I won't. Because I didn't do *any* of this for myself. I did this to save the life of a man I love. And if you want to know *why* or how, or any of the rest of it, you're going to have to send them away. Then you can decide whether you want to tell them or not."

Artemis nodded, her eyes unblinking, her jaw set. She felt a ferocity in her gaze that hadn't been there before. She sat a bit straighter, immobile. Resolute like a sphinx.

In the end, Artemis hadn't been doing any of this out of a sense of self-preservation.

Remember what you want to accomplish.

A small maxim that Helen had often uttered. Helen, in Artemis' opinion, would've been a world chess champion by now if she hadn't disappeared. If she hadn't been... taken.

Artemis blew air slowly, not having realized it was pent up in her lungs. But she stared directly at Mrs. Doler, a challenge in her eyes.

The older woman was frowning back, sizing up the younger woman.

Artemis had made an impression, that much was clear. But was it a *good* impression? Only time would tell.

Finally, the matriarch glanced towards the door. Both of her nephews were shaking their heads. But Doler said, "She's unarmed you said?"

Not-Glen nodded. Darren—but probably David—said, "Not a good idea. She'll talk. I guarantee it. You said we needed this done before Mr. Doler gets back."

But Mrs. Doler sniffed and raised a hand with a sort of regal pose. She extended her fingers—soft fingers. Fingers unaccustomed to callous or labor. "David," she said simply, her voice tense, "My husband is a vindictive man. I'm not. Hell," she added, muttering to herself as if venting for no other purpose than to release the irritation, "he wants to take the house in the proceedings... But, we'll handle this *my* way."

The off-duty cop frowned then sighed, approached his aunt, pulled his weapon from its holster, hesitated only briefly but then handed it to Doler.

Then, after another nod from their aunt, the two nephews slunk away, slipping back into the hall and closing the glass and wood door to the study behind them. Both men took a few steps into the atrium but then turned, watching attentively through the glass like hawks studying prey.

Their faces were distorted by the thick glass, and Artemis looked away from them.

Her eyes settled on the gun clutched in Doler's hand, pointed at Artemis' head.

"Well?" Doler said softly, weapon aimed. "Tell me *why*. Why should I trust you?"

Artemis exhaled faintly. She swallowed and said, "A woman kidnapped two people I care for. Very deeply. She gave me an ultimatum. That's why."

"Start from the beginning. We have time."

Artemis shook her head though, fiercely. "That's just it. We don't. *They* don't. We're all running out of time." She steadied herself, inhaling deeply, and then said, "But fine. I'll tell you everything. But then I have an offer."

"What sort of offer?"

"A deal," Artemis said simply. "I'll give you what you want. Then you give me what I want."

Improvisation. The gambit played. She'd risked it all. Would the opponent bite?

Mrs. Doler said, "You don't know what I want."

"I do. I know you want the Aristocrat in jail."

"No. I don't."

"You... you don't?"

"I don't want him in jail, dear. Whoever did this. Whoever took my angel from me, who broke our family into shattered pieces... I don't want him in jail. Do you understand?"

Artemis swallowed faintly. Her eyes darted to the faces visible through the thick glass. But she bobbed her head a single time. "I understand."

"Good. So let's say, for a moment, though I don't trust you, I do believe you. You think you can solve this case? Twenty years, Artemis. Twenty years is a long time."

Artemis hesitated, biting her lip. "I'm willing to try. What other choice is there?"

Mrs. Doler smiled now. A crocodile's grin. And for a moment, Artemis was reminded of Supervising Agent Grant.

The older woman leaned her head back against the headrest, nodded and said. "Not much choice at all. So go on, dear. Tell me *everything*." A pause, a faint shrug of elegant shoulders beneath purple silk. "And then we can decide what to do with you."

Chapter 7

Forester frowned from his position amidst the trees behind the large mansion.

Something had gone wrong.

He rubbed at the palm of his scarred hand, the white, pale rope of skin moving up his palm, up his arm and disappearing under his dark sleeve.

Cameron "BamBam" Forester wasn't the fighter he used to be. But his instincts, developed over a childhood of living rough and on the fun side of the law, told him now would be a good time to skedaddle.

And yet he didn't.

He stayed, behind the house, eyes on the silhouettes through the window of the faux-stone turret. He'd spotted the additional figures a few minutes too late to warn Artemis.

And now, he spotted the slim silhouette of a young woman wearing a red dress moving past the window, sitting in a chair. Two large men were in the room.

As well as the mark.

"Shit," he said. His thumb continued to rub against his palm in rapid, circular motions. His dark hair was tussled by the breeze, and no matter how often he attempted to slick it back, his fringe seemed to have a mind of its own.

Not quite unlike the man it belonged to. Forester still wasn't quite sure *how* he'd ended up in the FBI. Auntie Shauna was a big part of it.

His fighting career, another part of it.

Equally uncertain was why in the double hells was he angling outside some godforsaken window in big-town yuckity-yuckville waiting for some girl who didn't even like him much.

Now that was the million-dollar question.

He leaned against the rough bark of the prickling fir, his feet splayed in the detritus of scattered pine needles turning from green to orange and dollops of lichen and moss torn from the ground and scattered by the traversing of squirrels.

These small creatures, with their bushy tails, were also frightened of him. Watching from dark corners of different boughs.

And they had every right to *be* scared.

Forester had killed more than his fair share of the critters as a youth. Pellet guns and slingshots were secondary in choice to a good ol' slung bottle or rock.

His aunt had been mortified when she'd found out what Cameron had been up to. Killing small animals, she'd warned him, was never a good sign.

Military school hadn't stuck. That particular incident with one of the more irritating instructors' convertibles had been a close shave.

Forester hadn't *meant* to dismantle the vehicle and rebuild it on top of the glass roof above the swimming pool. He certainly hadn't meant for the glass to *break* and the convertible to fall *into* said pool while some of the underclassmen had been doing laps.

Forester winced.

None of his co-conspirators at the time had ratted him out, and so he'd been expelled rather than imprisoned.

His aunt hadn't found it amusing.

Forester shifted again, and the pine needles crackled underfoot. He felt a faint trickle of sweat along his cheek, but then reached up and realized a small bug must've climbed off the tree onto his face. He flicked the critter free... but didn't stop to crush it.

Killing small animals just didn't have the same *appeal* as it used to.

Not after *her*.

She had changed everything.

He'd often thought he'd end up behind bars. Or on some most wanted list. At times, he'd even aspired to see how high he could climb the ladder of the federals' favorite wish list.

But in his twenties, during the start of his fighting career, she'd wandered onto the scene.

And everything had changed.

Never before had a good-for-nothing done such a one-eighty to impress a girl. It was her eyes he remembered most...

Forester allowed a ghost of a smile beneath the tree. And he felt a strange emotion rising in him, thick in his throat.

He didn't often *feel* emotion... and yet for some reason, the memory of her brought it all back. He'd never known what love was.

Never experienced it. Certainly not the emotion involved.

But something about her had broken it all down. And now...

He let out a little sigh. He supposed she was the reason he was standing outside the big ol' house waiting to get his ass thrown in jail.

But he couldn't just leave.

As much as it might have been the smart move...

"God dammit, she doesn't even like you..." he said, trying to speak on behalf of his more rational side. "She's *scared* of you, dunce."

He frowned at this characterization.

It was true. He knew it was true. She'd essentially said as much. Artemis Blythe was *not* the woman he'd lost.

And yet...

The resemblance was so damn uncanny it sometimes made his skin crawl.

And there she was, in a red dress that fit in all the right ways, with those beautiful eyes that seemed to be peering from a misty past...

And there she was again... In trouble.

The last time, he hadn't been quick enough.

He hadn't known she was in trouble... not until too late. And then, when he'd found out, he'd been too damn slow.

Seven years ago. It had all changed.

He wasn't going to be late a second time.

At this thought, a strange fire kindled in his chest. He began to march forward like a man possessed. Like a man under the influence. And it was an influence of a type—intoxicating to his core.

But he was a sober-minded as a priest.

He marched towards the large house. Scowling as he did, his hand dropping to the weapon on his hip. His fingers touched the cold metal. His scarred hand bunched into a fist.

If he had to drop bodies, so be it.

If they were threatening her life in *any* way, he'd rip their throats out.

The last time...

God dammit... He pictured the blood. His stomach twisted. So much blood. So very much... And the taunting letters written in her blood, scrawled across the bathroom mirror, just for him to find.

He picked up the pace now, approaching the window. It wasn't until he was a few paces away that he thought he might fling himself bodily through the glass.

It also wasn't until he braced himself, ducking his head and tucking against his shoulder that he realized the room was empty.

He froze.

Standing in the dark, in the chill air, listening to the moan of wind through the surrounding trees. His eyes flicking along towards the other houses in the gated community and tracking the ridges of the tall, black fence encircling the space.

And then... a creak. A sound. Voices.

A long beam of orange light through a slit in an opening door spread across the cobblestone walkway outside the front door. The stretch of light grew, ensnaring the walkway entirely.

He cursed, ducking to the side, and pressing his back against the red brick wall. He stared towards the light, breathing slowly.

Behind him, he heard a faint whir and glanced back, eyes narrowed. A small golf cart with glowing headlights speeding by on dirt trails meandering around the houses.

Security.

Golf-cart security.

He watched as the small trolley passed and then returned his attention to the voices.

He detected her voice instantly, as if his very soul were primed to catch it. "I'll get you what you need," said Artemis, her voice shaking only slightly. He knew the sound. She was on the verge of a panic attack.

He felt a flicker of concern, of fear.

Emotions that were so foreign to him. Emotions he hadn't known a sociopath's brain could conjure. Emotions he hadn't experienced until he'd turned twenty. And then... emotions that had vanished seven years ago.

And now they were back.

Like a junkie's favorite fix once more found on a bumper corner.

He listened as Artemis said, "But you have to keep to the deal."

A pause. A faint clearing of a throat, and then a supercilious voice that made Forester bristle, "We'll see, Ms. Blythe. And remember, I hold all the cards."

Another exchange. This time one he couldn't quite hear. His back pressed to the brick wall, he eased forward, his cheek scraping the red stone as he tried to ease around the side of the house.

But just as quickly, he heard footsteps.

Shadows moving across the open doorway of light spread along the cobblestones.

A second later... a whirring sound.

Whirring... what was—

"Er, excuse me?"

A voice. Not from around the front of the house. But from behind Forester.

Chapter 8

Forester tensed, frozen in place.

A loud, pronounced swallowing noise. "E-excuse me!" the voice said, even louder.

Forester turned slowly, eyes narrowed like a snake's. He was *not* in the mood for distractions. Especially not from some damn rent-a-cop.

The mayor of rent-a-copsville was standing in front of the small golf cart he'd been puttering around in. The man was built like a scarecrow. Thin, with oversized sleeves that flapped in the faint breeze. He had a pencil-thin mustache and flashing white teeth which were on display due to the perfect circle his mouth had formed.

The small man was at least a foot shorter than Forester and had to tilt his head up to stare. To the little fellow's credit though, he didn't back away at the sight of Forester. And, standing ten paces away, stun gun in hand, he was pointing the weapon directly at Forester's chest.

"Don't move!" the little man exclaimed in a squeaking voice.

Forester had to admire the courage. But his admiration was short-lived, replaced rapidly by irritation. The front door, around the side of the large house, had just slammed.

Time was ticking. Where the hell was Artemis? What had happened with those two thugs the mark had sprung on her?

Forester's back was to the red brick wall now. The windows above the two of them were too high for the rent-a-cop to see through.

Forester just glared at the small man and his stun gun.

"Who are you?" the security officer snapped. The squeak had faded from his voice, and his small mustache quivered.

In fact, most of him was quivering. But again, in a show of impressive courage, the small figure didn't back away, didn't say *anything*. He just lingered, finger on the trigger of his stun-gun, his mouth pressed in a thin, grim line.

"Not now," Forester said, allowing a growl to creep into his voice. He began to turn to glance around the side of the building again.

"Hands where I can see them!" the small man piped up, speaking in a cadence as if he were reading off a cue card.

Forester turned again slowly, his eyes lingered on the man, and then he raised a hand. "That the new T-series?"

The small man glanced down, then up again, his hands trembling.

Forester shook his head. "Gotta flip the safety, my guy. Those new issues are locked up tighter than—"

"Hands up!" the security guard, however, glanced at the side of the stun gun, realized Forester was telling the truth, and flipped the safety. He then swallowed, his Adam's apple bobbing.

"Right, right," Forester said, still half listening to the footsteps around the side of the house, but momentarily distracted. "When you pull the trigger, you're gonna wanna squeeze gently, got it? If you pull too hard, it'll jerk and the double prongs with the wired tethers will go wide, okay? So here... wanna try? Aim right for my chest. Not my head—my head is too small'a target."

Now, the security guard just looked confused.

Forester faced the small man, watching him closely. Forester could feel his irritation being replaced by something a bit more predatory. It was in his voice, a husky sound. In the way his hands balled at his sides, refusing to lift and follow the man's orders.

Forester's eyes narrowed, and his head tilted ever so slightly as he studied the smaller man like a lion eyeing a slab of steak.

The guard must've spotted something he didn't like in Forester's gaze, because the man let out another squeak and took a step back. He stumbled into his golf cart. Forester, noticing the jerking motion, simply stepped to the side.

There was a zipping sound, and the two electrocuting prongs shot past his shoulder, hitting harmlessly against the wall. Forester nodded slowly and looked up.

The guard, holding the stun gun, which was now useless, gaped, lower lip trembling. Forester pointed at the ground. "See—that's why you gotta squeeze gentle. Now, how about this. How about you get in that little go-cart of yours and scoot on outta here. And I? Know what I'll do? Nothing. I won't draw my own gun. I won't come at you and tie you into a pretzel. I won't even take this..." he scuffed his foot through the prongs in the dirt, "as an insult. Just more as... instructional. Sound fair?"

Another squeak.

Forester, sighing and deciding that the more verbose approach was overkill, simply said, "Scram, buddy."

And the small guard backed away. Forester shook his head, turning.

And the guard was on him. The little guy finding more courage than ninety percent of the cage fighters Forester had fought. The attack was heralded only by the faint flurry of rapid footfalls, a desperate shout, and the sound of a night-stick whistling through the air.

The little guy was too short to aim for Forester's head, so instead, he tried to strike the back of Forester's leg, trying to cause him to buckle. Just like in a training manual.

Except the strength behind the blow was lacking, and the strike to Forester's leg should've gone for the joint but instead ricocheted off the meat of his calf.

Forester grunted, turning now.

And he lost his temper.

But Forester could *control* his anger. He was a sociopath, not a rage monster. And as concerned as he was for Artemis, by the sound of things, they were letting her go.

And this little guy had guts.

Instead of striking him, Forester simply lifted him off the feet by the scruff of his neck. The security guard was yelling, swinging his night-stick again, this time aiming for Cameron's head. But the bad-boy fed caught the club, tossed it into the bushes and then, after two long strides, placed the small, courageous guard on top of his golf cart.

"Stay!" Forester snapped, pointing a finger and glaring. Then, to make sure this happened, Forester bent over, snatched the discarded stun gun and used the two tethers on either side to wrap around the guard's wrist.

The rent-a-cop protested violently, but Forester's hands moved deftly. He tied the small guy's wrist to the handle on the white plastic ceiling.

Now, spluttering, the guard protested, "Let me down!"

Forester did not.

Instead, leaving the guard tied to the roof of his own golf cart, Forester turned and began to move around the side of the house now. In the distance, down the path, he spotted where Artemis was heading towards the front gate, pretending as if she'd exit that way.

The plan had been to meet back at the large breaker box.

But she was still within eyesight of their mark, and she clearly knew it.

The older woman was standing on the porch steps, one arm akimbo, eyes narrowed beneath her short-cut white fringe.

And quiet enough so only the two men behind her could hear—along with any eavesdroppers in the bushes—the woman said, "Follow her. Find out what she really wants..."

One of the men, a clean-cut fellow with bowling balls for biceps, said, "Why are we letting her go?"

"Because, David," she said quietly, "If she can give me what she offered, then all of this will be worth it." Mrs. Doler turned to examine the two young men with neat haircuts and polo shirts. She said, softly, "This doesn't get out. To anyone. Don't breathe a word."

"Course not," said the other guy.

"Now please, follow her."

Mrs. Doler swept past them, a look of utmost concern etched across her features. She moved back into the large house with hasty motions. The door shut behind her, a large, brass lion on the door now catching the faint light from the bulb above the porch.

The two men on the steps shared a look, frowned, and one of them muttered, "I don't trust her."

"Nah," said the one with the biceps, David. "Let's go talk to her ourselves, huh? The old-fashioned way."

Both of them shared a grim, dark look, suggesting *old-fashioned* wasn't a euphemism for minding their P's and Q's.

Chapter 9

Mrs. Doler's two thugs moved down the stairs, taking long strides.

Artemis, who'd reached the end of the small street glanced back. The polo-shirts kept moving, faster now.

Forester scowled, stepping from behind the house.

But suddenly, Artemis broke into a sprint, disappearing around another house.

The two pursuing men cursed and broke into twin sprints as well. Forester was a good fifty yards away. And they were *fast*.

Forester stiffened briefly and cursed.

He could run after them...

Or...

The men were calling out, but Artemis didn't return. Now the two men reached the end of the street, disappearing after Forester's grudging consultant.

And Forester reached a decision. Two stumbling steps after the men were discarded in favor of an about-turn.

Forester veered around the side of the house now, instead, hastening towards where the golf cart was still parked, the dinky little headlights glaring.

Those weren't the only glaring thing, however, as the guard tied to the roof gave Forester a deathly glare.

"Let me down, this instant!"

His hand was still tied with wire. And by the look of things, the knot had only tightened. Which, in a way, was the point of the dummy slipknot Forester had used.

Now, he called out, "Sorry guy!"

And he flung his large frame into the small golf-cart seat. Crammed in, knees nearly to his chest, Forester floored the pedal.

The small thing, as he'd spotted earlier, had some real get-up-and-go. And now, the golf cart whizzed around the side of the house.

Forester doubled the speed of the fleeing men.

He glared over the cheap, plastic steering wheel, hands white where he gripped tightly. Meanwhile, his siren blared from the rooftop.

Not exactly a *conventional* siren.

He winced. "Sorry, guy!" he called out. "I swear, I didn't mean to do this."

A hand was flapping in front of the plastic sheet windshield, waving desperately about in an attempt to gain his attention. He winced at the fluttering fingers which accompanied some impressively high-pitched shrieks.

"I know it *looks* intentional..." he said, muttering to himself now, and veering down the street. The small little electric-powered motor whirring beneath him.

He'd thought he'd been clever. Placing the small guy on a roof, tying him there. No way to reach his radio. No way to drive the golf cart for help.

But now...

The small fellow was slowing him. Weighing down the machine as he sped hastily forward, racing in pursuit of the men in the distance.

It was testament to his aunt's influence that he didn't simply reach up, unknot the tethers and allow the burden slowing his vehicle to fly off.

Instead, his attention was caught by the figures near the tall, black-spiked, ornate fence circling the properties.

The two men had backed Artemis into a corner and were menacing her. The one with the bowling ball biceps had stepped forward, and his hand lingered on a weapon at his hip. His other hand extended, palm flat as if to hold her at bay by sheer force of will.

The second man had taken up a flanking position, cutting Artemis off from any attempt to run around the other way.

All three of the figures were breathing heavily, sweaty and panting between brief bouts of conversation.

Now, Biceps stepped forward again. His hand catching Artemis by the arm, holding tight.

"Nope," Forester muttered beneath his breath.

He'd been slowing the golf cart, but the moment he spotted the physical touch, he floored the pedal again. The guard on the roof yelled incoherently.

All three figures by the fence looked sharply over, the two thugs whirling around, hands pulling weapons from concealed holsters.

The guns didn't make it *out* of the holsters fully, though.

Artemis and her two accosters just stared, quizzical. Their heads tilted slowly, and one at a time, they glanced at each other, as if making sure they were all seeing the same thing.

Now, Forester's temporary captive was screaming from the top of the speeding cart. Forester picked up the pace, his own weapon held in hand but hidden behind the console. He didn't want to get into a shootout with these guys in the middle of Fancyville.

Artemis was the first to realize what was happening. Her eyes widened in horror—those same mismatched eyes as always. She stared at Forester with an expression of sheer disbelief, her jaw opening, closing, then opening again.

She shot a helpless little look towards the two thugs.

Now, both of them seemed to realize that the man trapped on top of the roof wasn't *willingly* participating in this charge towards them.

Weapons rose. Both men's hands leapt out. Their voices boomed. "Slow the vehicle! Hands where we can see them!"

Shouting far too loud, attempting to control the space with their voices.

But Forester had gone through the same damn training. Not just in Quantico but also as a kid. Whenever a cop yelled, it meant they wanted to gain control. Which also meant they didn't have it yet.

And so Forester didn't slow. They sped forward. Hit a small incline in the grass framing the dirt path, leapt over the divot, and—back wheels spinning and scattering turf—they flew through the air and slammed into the fence.

They'd missed the thugs by a good two feet. But Forester was already moving. The golf cart's top speed hadn't been *that* impressive.

And though the plastic sheet windshield was cracked, Forester was good to go.

He felt something warm on his lip as, dazedly, he pushed out of the vehicle, blood trickling down his face.

The guard on top of the roof was breathing heavily, murmuring prayers under his breath, and trying to cross himself with the hand still tethered to the cold, and now very much bent, plastic roof.

But Forester didn't have time to apologize to his temporary passenger. He'd pushed out of the golf cart, but had only taken two steps before large hands snagged at him and flung him against the black fence.

"What the hell do you think you're doing?" One of the men snapped. He shoved at Forester with two flat hands.

And that's when Cameron's instincts took over.

He ducked the shove, twisting at the hips. His fist caught the man in the gut. Forester was still breathing heavily, still bleeding from the nose, but now the pain was secondary, the dizziness forgotten.

The second thug, the one with the biceps, named David, came lunging in with a shout. He'd holstered his weapon, seemingly to reach for cuffs, but now he swung a fist at Cameron's head and darted back just as quickly.

His other hand scrambled for his weapon.

Forester's own gun was in hand first, though.

"Nu-uh," he said slowly, shaking his weapon side to side. "Drop it."

David stared, mouth hanging open. His eyes fixated on the gun, then darted back up to Forester—his eyes narrowed.

"I said *drop it*," Forester snapped.

But then Artemis called out, "Behind you!"

Forester turned in time to catch a fist to the nose. He was sent reeling by the second thug. David managed to pull his gun but Forester used the momentum from being sent tumbling and careened into David.

The two of them grunted as they hit the grass, Forester on top. He took the gun.

David yelled.

Forester threw it over the fence, and shoved off the man on the ground, planting his large, calloused palm against David's chest and using it for leverage. A whooshing sound of breath being released accompanied Forester's shoving motion.

Forester spun on his back heel, sending his opposite foot out, slamming it into the abdomen of the man who'd struck him from behind.

"My nose was already bleeding!" Forester yelled in frustration. Crimson ribbons were now pouring down his upper lip.

He then snagged at Artemis and pulled her towards the golf cart, between the two men he'd downed. Mid-step, he pivoted, "One second, sorry," he muttered to Artemis while he spun around with a spinning back heel and *kicked* the second thug's gun out of his hand.

A yelp of pain, and the gun went arcing through the air, clattering off the fence.

The two men were both gasping, groaning and trying to push off the grass and rise to their feet. Artemis was shaking badly under his grip. She kept staring at the men, her eyes darting back along the path in the direction she'd come from.

"Shit..." she was whispering. "Forester... I... I..."

"Tell me later!" he said firmly.

He reached up, tore the tethers with one meaty fist, and then dragged the guard off the roof. He was gentle about it. He'd grown to like the courageous little fellow—something about the tenor of his shrieks.

Forester patted the flabbergasted guard down, adjusted his lapels, patted him on the head and said, "Thanks, guy."

And then Forester led Artemis into the golf cart, and he floored it again.

This time, he decided, they'd circle to the opposite side of the fence. They could use the mobile golf cart to set up an egress at any point in the fence now.

As they sped away, Forester reached down and flicked a silver button, turning the headlights off and, hopefully, he decided, obscuring them further.

He glanced back to see one of the thugs on his feet, wobbly attempting to help the other to rise.

He exhaled in a long sigh, then shot Artemis a look.

Pale-faced, frightened, she looked the worse for wear. Concern pulsed in his chest.

Focus. He thought to himself.

"You okay?" he said. Not because it was normally a natural instinct to inquire about another's well-being, but because habit had built the question up over the years.

She just shook her head, setting her lips in a thin, grim line.

"What happened?"

"Nothing good."

"Huh."

"Where were you!" she said.

"Outside. Should I have come through the window?"

"No... no, sorry, I'm being unreasonable. Thank you, by the way." She shot a look back as the two of them sped up a dirt trail under some trees and past a fountain.

"Yeah... yeah sure," he said conversationally. "Say..." he frowned. "What was the old lady talking about when you were leaving? Do we have access to her husband or not?"

"No," Artemis said simply. She bit her lip. "Not unless I do something first."

"A favor? Damn... she figured you out, then?"

"Not only that... they're running my face on the news, Cameron."

He winced.

"That's not all," she said slowly, her voice shaking. The wind picked up, ushered through the doorless, open flanks of the golf cart. The wheels whirred along the dusty ground.

"What's the favor?" Forester asked.

"I have to solve a decades-old cold case. And if I don't, she's going to tell her husband everything. Tell the cops. The feds..." Artemis bit her lip, her tone grim, her hands still shaking horribly where she'd clasped them in her lap. "And then Jamie and Sophie will die."

Chapter 10

Artemis hadn't been sure where to start investigating a cold case, but she supposed a diner on the outskirts of Pinelake was as good a place as any.

She shivered as she sat in a window seat in the back of the diner. The crack beneath the windowsill allowed a chill breeze to sweep through the dank, dingy restaurant. The scent of reheated potatoes and macaroni salad lingered on the air.

Artemis rubbed at her arms, still wearing her stupid red dress and wishing she'd taken the time to head back to the motel they'd been staying at.

But that was the one thing they didn't have much of. Time. The clock was ticking.

In less than four days, her father needed to be *out* of prison, or else...

She swallowed, feeling a lump in her throat and not wanting to contemplate the *or else*.

"Tell me again why we're doing this?" Forester muttered darkly from where he sat across from her in the booth. The large man's knees didn't quite fit beneath the hefty, plastic table, which was bolted to the floor. He hunched over, looking miserable, his features illuminated by the bluish glow from his laptop.

Forester didn't seem to mind the cold ushering through the window.

In fact, there weren't many physical discomforts that seemed to bother the ex-fighter. Now, calloused fingers were tapping mercilessly against the keyboard.

"Have they locked you out?" Artemis asked quickly.

The agent grunted, then shook his head. "Nah... Dawkins didn't recognize me, I guess. I'm in the clear. Speaking of which..." Forester frowned, glancing off towards the side where his phone was now buzzing against the table.

Artemis glanced towards the device. The name on the phone simply read, *Auntie*.

She swallowed, stared. "Shouldn't you pick that up?"

Forester shrugged. "Nah. More suspicious if I did." He returned his attention to the computer and reached up to scratch at his chin. "Huh," he muttered faintly. "Alright then."

"Alright what?"

"We're in..."

He turned the computer a bit, and forced Artemis to lean forward across the table to peer at the device. As she did, she adjusted the neckline on her dress, which felt as if it were a bit too low for modesty's sake.

Her arms were cold where they rested against the plastic table, and goosebumps rose along her forearm from the breeze.

A voice was calling out in the diner, and a waitress, with golden dye in otherwise pale hair, tottered over, snatched a tray and moved towards the only other patrons in the place. A small family that had stopped off on what looked like the final leg of some road trip—evident by bags under the eyes, disheveled clothing and an all-around listlessness in the two parents and two kids.

Artemis' gaze had moved to the computer, now, though, and she frowned as she scanned hastily through the open files.

"Unsub 23?" Artemis murmured.

"Unknown subject," Forester shot back. "At least... I think so." He scratched at his head. "Huh. Probably shoulda paid closer attention during lectures. Anyway, don't click anything. Wade'll be pissed."

"As in Agent Wade?" Artemis blinked, then looked over the top of the computer. "We're not using *his* account, are we?"

"Hey, hey. Don't give me that look. Not my fault his password is password spelled backwards. Natural selection at work. The weak must die."

"You're an odd man, Agent Forester."

"Yeah, well—shit... why doesn't she just stop calling me." He glared at the phone. It was buzzing again.

Artemis and Forester both stared at it now, both equally quiet, like some bomb disposal crew waiting for a fuse to ignite.

After a sigh, Forester reached down, snagged the device and lifted it.

His entire demeanor shifted. It was like watching a chameleon change its scales. An instantaneous transformation. One moment, grim, concerned and sarcastic. The next, chipper, upbeat and energetic.

"Hey auntie, how's life? Miss me?"

He'd clicked on speaker phone, and extended it so Artemis could hear.

"Cameron?" snapped the familiar and severe voice of Supervising Agent Shauna Grant.

In her mind's eye, Artemis conjured an image of the single, sixty-something, elegant woman. The pale-haired agent often wore emerald earrings that matched the hue of her piercing gaze. Shauna Grant was a woman who demanded results, and she didn't suffer fools lightly.

Forester played the fool, but his aunt knew what he really was.

And now, it was clear in her tone, she wasn't in the mood for jokes. "Where are you, Cameron?" she snapped.

"Strip club," he said lazily. "Er... sorry, I mean paragliding in the alps. You know, the usual."

"Where are you really, Cameron. *Now.*"

A long sigh. "You worried about me? I'm at a diner. Helping Artemis Blythe escape the cops and try to catch a decades-old killer."

"It's not funny, Forester. Where are you really?" A pause. Then Shauna quickly cut-in, "Hang on. Are you *actually* with Artemis Blythe?"

"Yup. She's right here. Wanna chat?"

Artemis just stared at Forester wide-eyed and stunned. What was he doing? The last thing they needed was for the FBI to know the two of them were together. Forester was committing career suicide. Hell... he would get his own ass chucked in lock-up.

But then, Agent Grant snapped, "Stop teasing and be serious. Tell me where you are. I'll send Desmond to pick you up."

"Told you," Forester said lazily. "Strip club."

"When's the last time you saw Ms. Blythe?"

Artemis shivered. Something about the way Agent Grant said her name gave Artemis the chills.

"Dunno... Sometime. Around. *Dunno.* She really kill Agent Butcher?" Forester said, and now there was something in his voice. Not playful or pretend but grim.

Shauna cleared her throat. "We're still looking into it. As you can imagine, the deputy director is playing things close to the vest. I... I'm sorry, Cameron. I know you and Agent Butcher were close once upon a time."

"Yeah... yeah, it's rough." Forester said quietly.

Artemis just stared at him, realizing just how odd the man across from her was. He was hitting all the right cues. And in anyone else's case, she would've instantly sympathized. But it was testament to his skill at dishonesty that she couldn't tell if he was lying or being sincere.

He slipped so seamlessly from one to the next that it gave her whiplash. She'd grown up with a psychopath who'd taught her how to read the emotions in others like a meteorologist commenting on the weather in another country.

She'd learned how to read the smallest twitch of an eyebrow, the closing of hands, the shifting of feet.

All of it made sense. At least... for *most* people.

But Cameron Forester was *not* most people, and he proved it even now as he chatted with his aunt, lying about being with Artemis insofar as he was lying about *not* being with her. It was enough to make her head spin.

Now, as she stared at Forester, she realized something else.

The only times she ever *truly* believed he was telling the truth was when he looked at her. Not when he spoke. Not really in anything he said. But when his eyes settled on her, when he thought she wasn't looking especially, and he just watched her.

Sometimes he ogled. Other times he tried to stare down her dress or at her legs. It all made her distinctly uncomfortable, but also... in a way...

No.

No, it wasn't worth considering anything *beyond* the discomfort.

But there were other times. More often than the obnoxious ogling he seemed to engage in without an ounce of shame.

Times when he watched her, and there was only pain in his eyes. Grief and loss and longing... and sometimes, though not often, hope.

Faint prickles spread along her arms. How in the hell did she instill hope in a man like this? It didn't make sense, and she knew there were pieces of the puzzle she could place together. But she found she didn't want to.

She didn't want to read Forester. Didn't want to plumb the depths of this man.

No... best to leave things at surface level with the handsome, bedraggle-haired ex-cage-fighter.

And now, he was chatting amicably again, breezily saying, "It's fine, auntie. I'll swing by after the dance. Unless you want to stop by."

"Yes. I want to. Tell me the address. Desmond is on his way—don't leave."

"Don't gotta tell me twice," Forester said with a chuckle. "They got a buffet and everything." He rattled off an address, and Artemis wondered if it actually belonged to a strip club.

Again, with Forester, she really couldn't say one way or the other. She thought of him a bit like a wolf. A man that could occasionally *look* like a domesticated pet, in the right light, after a meal and a long run, but given enough time, the restlessness, the appetites would take over...

And he'd become dangerous again.

Forester bid farewell to his aunt, shut off the phone and then shot Artemis a look. "Well?" he said. "What do you think?"

She realized she'd been staring at his profile. She swallowed, looked quickly away and *absolutely* hated to realize she was blushing. What the hell was that about?

Her own blood vessels were now betraying her.

"Ummm... what? Sorry. Huh?"

"The unsub. The Aristocrat. What are you thinking?"

"Oh... uh, yeah, right." She shook her head, flustered and not understanding why. It was the exhaustion, she decided. The lack of sleep. The last few days living on the run. The chaos of it all—it was all getting to her. She shot a quick glance towards the diner's counter, seeking out any evidence of a freshly brewed pot of coffee.

Then, she said quickly, "I... I told Mrs. Doler I'd find who killed her daughter... but... twenty years is a long time."

"Might not even have all the files scanned," Forester said. "Some of the stuff from the field office in the city was a bit slower on the upload if I remember. But that was from something I worked only a decade or so ago. Not twenty years."

Forester leaned back, though it was difficult to maneuver in the booth for the lengthy fellow.

"So Doler agreed to give you her husband if you solve the case?"

"No," Artemis said quickly. "I... I told her that I wanted to speak with her husband about my father's living conditions. I wanted to get him some amenities in prison."

"She bought that?"

"I don't know. She was focused on the thought of finding out what happened to her daughter. It was all a bit of an emotional roller coaster."

"I'd say. Shit. So you solve the case, and she gives a sit down with the warden."

"Looks like it."

"Then what?"

Artemis just shook her head. "I don't really know. We still have to figure out how to leverage the warden to get Otto out of there."

"Yeah. Huh. Only a few days then to solve a cold case. Bit of an ask."

"Yeah. Tell me about it."

Forester was now playing with a plastic straw, blowing on it and causing it to roll across the table. He then placed his large, scarred hand on the opposite side of the straw and blew against his hand, causing the straw to travel backwards towards him from the reflected wind. It looked as if the straw were magically, on its own accord, moving.

It was a small, silly sleight-of-hand trick her father had often used to impress young women in hotel bars.

She frowned, finding it disconcerting to watch Forester utilize a trick her old man had often used.

She watched absentmindedly as the straw tumbled across the slick table, impeded only when it reached an old ketchup stain near Forester's arm.

"How much do you know about the Aristocrat," she said, still staring at the straw in motion.

The straw went suddenly still now as Forester used his breath to speak. "Not much," he said. "Way before my time."

"He kidnapped eight young women over the course of a decade."

"A decade? On this side or that side of twenty years?"

"He started thirty years ago," Artemis said. "The last person he took was Bella Doler. The warden's daughter. *That* was twenty years ago. And also, I'd guess, part of the reason for Mr. Doler's career shift from defense attorney to prison management."

"Gotcha..." Forester said, "So if this guy's an unsub..."

Artemis scrolled through the file on the computer screen, frowning as she did. "No suspects. A few people questioned, but all of them cleared." She scowled now, tapping a finger angrily against the computer screen. "I mean... what the hell. This guy wasn't even in the same *country* at the time of the kidnapping. Plus a mechanic by trade. And this guy... this guy was a pizza delivery driver. Who delivered to a house *two streets* away." She shook her head as she rapidly read through the file, her eyes dancing along the text.

Forester just watched her, speculative. "So you called this guy a kidnapper, not a killer."

Artemis sighed, nodding, closing her eyes now and preferring to use the information from memory. "Mhmm. No bodies were ever found."

"So... how do they know this Aristocrat *took* them? If they don't know who he is and don't know what happened to the victims..."

"He had a type," Artemis said quickly, glancing over. "Art students. Theater students. All of them pretty. Late teens, early twenties. Plus ..." She swallowed faintly, her eyes closing again as she allowed images to swim across her vision. "He used their blood in paintings."

"Hang on, what now?"

"He was a *very* good painter," Artemis said. "He would keep his victims for months... years sometimes completing his paintings. He'd use their blood in some of the pigments. And then drop the paintings off at various museums in the area."

Artemis' eyes snapped open, and she shrugged sheepishly at Forester. "Kinda gruesome, I know."

"So... how come they call him the Aristocrat?" Forester said, frowning.

"You really don't know much about this case, do you?"

"Like I said, it was before my time."

"Yeah, but... everyone tracked this thing. It made national news."

Forester snorted. "Trust me, Artemis, teenage Forester was a bit more interested in *local* news at the time. What street corners cops were cracking down on, for instance."

"Yeah... okay..." She nodded faintly, watching the man again. She sometimes forgot that Forester had a past. Hell, she sometimes forgot he'd been a child. Once upon a time, Cameron Forester had been a teenage troublemaker.

She shivered in sympathetic terror for the beat cop assigned within ten blocks of Cameron's address.

She said, "Well, they called him the Aristocrat because of the galas he sent the paintings to."

"I thought you said he put the paintings outside museums."

"Yeah, he did. But always when some event was taking place there, or near there. He wanted the social elite, the wealthy, the well-off to *see* his paintings. Kinda like getting validation from them. And also, *what* he painted."

"What did he paint?"

In response, Artemis clicked one of the evidence tabs, cycled through the images, expanded one and turned it so Forester could see.

He leaned in, eyebrow raised, studying the image on the screen.

Forester whistled slowly. "Shit... He is really good."

"Yeah. That was partly why so many people paid attention. We don't like thinking of killers as competent in anything but murder. It almost humanizes them to think of them as artists or painters. But this was the sort of thing he painted."

Artemis tapped the screen indicating a nearly photo-realistic oil painting with hundreds of figures dancing around a room. The era looked to be Victorian, judging by the outfits and chandeliers. As Artemis looked at the painting, the figures in it almost came to life, as if they were *actually* moving, twirling about.

At any moment, it felt as if one of the figures might pirouette up from the canvas, dancing off the screen.

There were *hundreds* of equally detailed figures in the painting, their faces all immaculately attended to. Artemis couldn't even *imagine* the amount of time something like this might have taken to complete.

For a few moments, almost a full minute, neither of them said a thing, both staring directly at the painting in some amount of reverence and awe.

It was testament to the effect art could possess that it had silenced Agent Forester.

"There's blood in that?" Forester said in manner of critique.

"Yeah. They found it in all the paintings."

"And... so what happened to the paintings? Eight of them, you said?"

"Seven. The eighth was never released. Bella Doler was taken, but no painting was ever found. It's always been something of a mystery."

"Huh, shit. But the paintings?"

"Evidence. Locked in evidence somewhere." Artemis shrugged. "There was a push by some fringe members to release the paintings to the public. Another group, equally vocal, wanted the paintings destroyed. A couple went missing... auctioned off, some say. But in the end, the remaining paintings were just locked away... left to gather dust."

"Wow. Any idea why he never completed his eighth painting?"

"No clue."

Forester sighed, leaning back. "So all the paintings look like this?"

"Here... click through. They're all photographed. But yeah, see? Victorian London. That's a tosher, there."

"A what?"

"A guy who'd descend into the sewers in the 1800s and look for jewels or coins before the tide would rise. Lantern around his neck, fear in his eyes."

Forester gave another low, impressed whistle as he studied this newest painting.

One by one they cycled through. All of the artwork showed the same time-period. Around the 1800s. Most of it showed aristocracy of some sort, but like the tosher, there were exceptions. Another was a blacksmith at a forge while a parade took place outside his window.

"Any clues in the paintings?" Forester said.

"You'd think so, but no one found any."

"What about you?"

Artemis was still studying the parade painting but then sighed, shaking her head. "Nothing... I don't know." She paused for a moment, feeling a wave of weariness wash over her. She moved from one painting to the next, her mind spinning.

She had to focus.

Thoughts of her father, even of Jamie and Sophie, of the strange woman, Fake Helen, who'd been working on behalf of her father...

It all needed to be shed like ballast.

She needed her mind clear. She scanned through the evidence—scant as it was—and moved over to witness testimony.

Most of the information was provided by family members who'd noticed their daughters missing. Mrs. Doler had even given a testimony.

Artemis shook her head slowly, muttering to herself. "Why did he stop... Twenty years ago. Think he's dead?"

"Could be. So where's the eighth painting? Where's Bella Doler?"

"Also dead?"

"So he kills her. Then dies himself? No one finds the bodies. No one finds the final painting?"

"Maybe... someone did find them? Just didn't tell anyone?"

Forester grunted. "If that's the case we're in trouble. Not sure Mrs. Doler is going to take *I don't know* as an answer."

"No... No, she didn't take it well the first time I tried that."

Artemis leaned back, shivering again from the breeze through the window. Her teeth pressed tightly together, and she frowned as she returned her attention to the computer screen. She tapped the arrow keys a few more times, then said, finally, "The first victim. Katya Solenger. She lived about thirty miles from here. Any way to find if her family is still there?"

"Yeah. Could do. Why? You wanna go speak with her parents?"

Artemis shook her head. "Katya lived with her grandparents. Parents weren't in the picture."

Forester frowned at this. He often had more visceral reactions when young women were the victims of crimes. She'd sometimes considered that *this* was why he'd joined the FBI. Whatever had happened to Cameron, it had left an indelible mark on him.

"Sure," Forester said, releasing a grateful sigh as he eased out of the cramped seating. "I can find where her grandparents live. Well... if they're still alive."

"Alright. At least we can start somewhere," Artemis said quickly, slipping out as well and shooting a lustful glance towards the fresh pot of steaming coffee on the counter. "Just, hang on. I'm going to grab a cup. You want any?"

"Nah. I'll meet you in the car—see if I can find the Solengers."

The two of them moved with purpose in their motions, a bit quicker than might normally have been expected in a diner.

But time was ticking, and to solve a decades-old case, Artemis needed all the help she could get.

Even of the caffeinated variety.

And as much as she wanted to focus on *other* things. She couldn't forget what was on the line if she failed.

CHAPTER 11

In Artemis' opinion, nursing homes came in two varieties. One type was the sort to plan activities every evening, to foster community, to serve decent—if not incredible—food, and to allow their tenants to decorate their new homes.

The other type looked like a hospital from hell.

Mrs. Solenger, the sole surviving relative of the Aristocrat's first victim, lived alone on the top floor of the *second* type of "care" facility.

Forester used his badge to lead the way past the check-in desk, approaching the elevator, which was framed by two plastic plants.

"I didn't realize fake plants came in that color," Artemis muttered, staring at the fake leaves, which looked brownish and wilted.

"Matches the walls," Forester muttered, wrinkling his nose and distastefully stepping over a stain on the ground that Artemis *hoped* was from some juice-box.

The elevator doors didn't ding, didn't flash, didn't give any indication the compartment had arrived until the two metal frames suddenly swung open with the speed of a guillotine.

Artemis and Forester stepped back as an older man wearing oversized glasses exited the elevator, moving with painstakingly slow motions. The man's walker nearly caught in a gap between the elevator doors, and Forester's hand shot out, catching the arm of the elderly fellow and guiding him towards the check-in desk.

Artemis frowned as the man hobbled away, then glanced back as Forester slipped into the elevator. She didn't join him.

He stared at her.

She stared back.

He glanced at the ground, up again. "Stairs then?"

She nodded.

He stepped out and the two of them moved towards the stairwell, marked by a gray door next to a streaky window.

"Sorry," Artemis muttered as they entered the stairwell, and the door swung shut behind them, sealing them off from any prying ears. "Just... Not sure I trust the elevator."

"Don't blame you. Pretty sure I spotted six safety violations just on my way in."

Artemis glanced back at Forester, who shook his head, frowned, and then began to lead the way up the stairs, taking them three at a time with his lengthy strides.

He moved quickly, and she followed, breathing in short gasps. Part of her routine in preparing for chess tournaments involved a morning workout, but of the two of them, Forester was certainly the more fit.

And it had been some time since she'd been able to stick to her usual routine.

She missed it.

"So Mrs. Solenger's husband passed when?" she said, breathing heavily between steps.

"Two years ago," Forester called back. "I'm *pretty* sure this is the right woman."

"Wait, hang on, I thought you were sure!"

"I mean, mostly. But records from back then are harder to associate with records from now. Social security number is the same. It's her," Forester said, frowning only for a moment but then flashing a thumbs up as he rounded the stairs.

The two of them moved in a hurry—after eight flights, Artemis began to wonder if perhaps they should've just taken the elevator. Her thighs hurt, and her breath came in quick puffs.

The two of them stood in a dingy hallway, outside a metal door. The metal was as cold as the hallway itself, and a flickering light in the center of the hall continued to sputter and fizz, casting eerie shadows over everything in view.

Forester leaned in, reading the name which was written in streaked marker on the masking tape strip left on the metal door.

The walls were bare, save some mold and water damage. Some of the paint was bubbling on the yellowish wall behind Artemis. The carpets were new, though, a strange distinction from the rest of the place's appearance, until Artemis got to wondering *why* a place like this had seen fit to change the carpets.

Forester's knuckles tapped at the door to the unit with *Donna Solengar* misspelled on the doorway.

After a few moments, a voice called out. "Coming!"

A pleasant, airy voice.

Artemis frowned briefly. A voice she thought she recognized. She shot a quick look towards Forester, and said, "Where was Mrs. Solenger from again?"

"Huh? Where? Seattle."

"No, what address?"

"Oh... like this place?"

"No!" Artemis said, quickly, a panic rising. She could hear footsteps coming towards the door now. Confident, sure-footed steps. Not the steps of an older woman living out her final days in this hellhole. But younger, spry footsteps. The steps of a dancer.

And now, Artemis' eyes were the size of saucers. She began slowly to back away, staring in horror at the door.

Forester was glancing at his phone, the illuminating glow from the device aiding to light up the hallway. After a few moments, he clicked his fingers. "Ah, there we go! She was on Staton Drive. Why?"

But Artemis just stared as the door opened slowly. "Coming, my darlings!" a cheerful voice called out. "Careful not to get smacked!"

Indeed, the door opened *outward* into the hall, instead of inward. It was only after the door began to open that Artemis spotted the hinges on the *outside* of the door.

But this eerie, little detail didn't change the fear suddenly sparking in Artemis's chest.

She remembered that voice, and the flamboyant person it belonged too. In fact, if she remembered correctly, this very person didn't *just* work as a catch-all coroner for the FBI, but occasionally, she volunteered her time to work with nursing home patients and the elderly.

Not for pay, but just out of a desire to be there for those who didn't have anyone else.

It made sense, then, Artemis decided, that Dr. Miracle Bryant—who still lived on the street where Mrs. Solenger used to reside—was now standing in the doorway, staring pleasantly out at the two of them.

Dr. Miracle Bryant blinked once, her eyes darting to Forester, lingering on his impressive biceps for a moment, but then flitting to his eyes.

The woman in the doorway wore sparkly-framed glasses and, even the way she'd opened the doorway had been done so with a flourish of her arm, like a ballerina curling her fingers.

The middle-aged woman wasn't what some might have called *thin*, but she wore her weight well, and the rosy glow tinging her dark features only added to the overall look of... *joy*.

Dr. Bryant's hair was no longer dyed pink, but instead now had taken on a lovely shade of mauve. The woman's eyes wrinkled in the corners, and she wore a bright pink shirt with bedazzled lettering which simply read, *You go girl!*

"Oh, what a nice and lovely surprise, Agent Forester!" Dr. Bryant began before she'd registered Artemis' presence. "See, look at that! I remembered your name and everything." She chuckled. "Thank you, Lord," she exclaimed, pumping her fist as if she'd just finished some race. But then, her eyebrows inched slightly up—perfectly plucked, arranged and partially sketched on—and she said, with something a bit more sly in her voice, "Where's pretty-eyes, huh?"

Forester blinked. "Er, oh. Agent Wade? Desmond's... I think he's at a strip club, actually."

Dr. Bryant frowned now, letting out a sigh. "Well," she said cautiously, "I suppose we all have our vices, don't we. God bless him." She reached out, patting Forester on the arm in a consoling way as if concerned that Wade visiting a strip club was a difficult thing for the tall sociopath.

And *that* was when Dr. Bryant's gaze landed on Artemis.

Chapter 12

Dr. Miracle Bryant stared at Artemis, blinked, and adjusted her sparkly glasses. The *You go girl!* in rhinestones across her pink sweater seemed like the *perfect* advice at that moment, but Artemis hadn't shaken her own shock quickly enough to make a dash for the stairwell.

Now, she found herself staring at Dr. Bryant, her mouth slightly unhinged.

Dr. Bryant stared back. For a moment, the two women mirrored each other in the way their arms suddenly dropped at their sides; their hands went limp. Dr. Bryant breathed slowly, a rattling breath. She swallowed, and her bedazzled sweater rose and fell with an ample bosom.

Then, the middle-aged coroner turned on her heel with a squawk, reached for the door and tried to slam it shut. Again, Artemis was impressed with how lithely the buxom woman moved. She snagged the door handle, trying to tug it closed, but Forester lunged forward, placing his foot in the way, preventing it from closing.

"Ack! Donna! Hide in the bathroom! Lock the door!" Dr. Bryant was shouting. She then snatched something off a desk inside the bedroom. A big, yellow phone-book. The type Artemis hadn't seen used in years by anyone from her generation.

But now, Dr. Bryant brandished the phone book at Forester, then at Artemis, shifting it back and forth, her eyes fierce behind those sparkling glasses.

"I know kung-fu!" she yelled, desperate. "Don't make me hurt you!"

Artemis sighed, Forester glanced over, shrugging sheepishly, his foot still wedged in the door.

Now, Dr. Bryant began stamping on Forester's foot. "Hey! Hey, stop that!" Forester yelped.

"Don't come near me, you traitor! Murderers! Help!" Dr. Bryant began shouting.

Forester let out a desperate sigh. Artemis was shaking her head at the sheer bad luck of the situation. Forester shoved into the room, though, hand darting out, clapping over Dr. Bryant's mouth and holding back a scream of, "Fiends! Desecrat—Mumpfh!"

Now, Forester pushed the older woman gently into the room, while still holding his hand over her mouth. He looked sheepish and was muttering like the engine of a motorboat, "I'm sorry. Sorry. Sorry—yah, stop licking my hand!"

Artemis followed quickly, her stomach twisting in horror at the situation. She slipped into the room, glancing quickly over her shoulder.

No one had reacted to the noise.

Perhaps no one had heard.

Or... a more grim interpretation. Perhaps such sounds were commonplace in a nursing home like this.

Artemis quickly shut the door behind her with a faint *click* and spun around, her back to the cool metal, facing the room.

Most of the small room resembled a hospital. A single room with a cot in one corner and a lumpy, old couch in another. There was evidence in the form of a floor-set litter box and tabby fur on a couch that some *other* creature lived in this space with the usual denizen, but there was currently no sign of the cat.

A very old woman, with thin strands of hair, was sitting upright in her bed, under piles of blankets, ignoring the entire scene and murmuring to herself as she did a sudoku puzzle.

Dr. Bryant was continuing to swat at Forester with her phone book while licking at his hand. Forester yanked his fingers away. "Gross!" he yelled. Then he was clobbered on the nose with the phone book.

He grunted, stumbling back and hitting the wall.

Most of the room was typical. But a couple of posters on the walls, Artemis guessed, were the contributions of their phone-book-wielding aggressor.

Both of the visible posters were motivational. One simply had the phrase, "*You can do it!*" With a woman wearing a red bandanna flexing her arm.

The other motivational poster... wasn't so much *motivational* as ... odd. It simply read, *Jesus Shaves!* Depicting a bearded man using whisker trimmers. In text beneath the image though, there was small type that described how every cent made from the sale of such a poster, and every person who donated hair, would be used to purchase or create wigs, toupees and the like for the elderly who couldn't afford their own.

For some reason, this seemed *exactly* like the sort of cause Dr. Bryant and her mauve hair might be involved in.

"Stop, please!" Artemis was protesting.

Forester was now defending himself against more phone-book blows. Wincing and stumbling back under the attack.

Dr. Bryant didn't stop. Instead, she redoubled her efforts. "You won't do me like you did that fed!" she called out in desperation. "Donna! Hide! Run!"

Donna, meanwhile, tugged a tongue out the side of her lips in focus, hesitated, leaned in, and scratched a number with a small, orange pencil into her sudoku booklet. She nodded to herself, grinning happily.

"We didn't kill anyone!" Artemis protested, trying to step between Miracle and Forester.

But she received a blow to the shoulder for her efforts, which sent her reeling back into Cameron. Forester caught her, his large hands gripping her shoulders before she toppled over the lumpy couch. She hesitated for a moment, breathing heavily, his hands still resting on her.

Just as quickly, though, a tingle going along her arms, she pushed away from Cameron, shaking her head hurriedly, her features flushed.

Dr. Bryant had taken this brief reprieve to retreat back to the bed and stand, phone-book raised, eyes narrowed behind sparkling glasses, like some guardian angel in a defensive posture by her charge.

"I bind thee in the name of the Lord!" she called out in an imitation of a booming, revival-preacher's voice. Then, when nothing seemed to happen, Miracle Bryant muttered, "Shit." Then winced and muttered an apology to the air, crossing herself with her free hand, and hefting her phone-book while wearing the grim countenance of someone destined for a last stand.

Forester was massaging his nose. Artemis stepped away from him and his warm hands. She wished suddenly she didn't *know* the temperature of his hands. Shit.

She didn't apologize for the expletive. Instead, she began to speak, but Forester beat her to it, his voice somewhat petulant as he gingerly pressed at his nose. "They teach you all that *bind thee* business in kung-fu, huh?"

Miracle glared. "Don't mock me, murderer!"

"We didn't kill anyone!" Artemis exclaimed in desperation. She then hesitated, glanced at Forester, and added, "Er... recently. Or... illegally. I think." She winced, realizing the hedging likely wasn't much helping their cause.

She approached Dr. Bryant, hands out in a pleading gesture. "I didn't kill those people. Please, I know you don't believe me. But it's true!"

Dr. Bryant swallowed faintly, clearly afraid as her eyes darted back and forth between Artemis and Forester. Her gaze lingered on Artemis for a moment, staring at her.

Artemis remembered her initial impression of Dr. Bryant had been a positive one. The woman didn't just march to the beat of her own drum but pirouetted to the cadence of an orchestra only she could hear. But also, she was very good at her job.

Artemis had always admired competence in others.

In addition, despite herself, Artemis couldn't help but *trust* Dr. Bryant. It wasn't anything about the woman's personality, ostentatious hair color or motivational slogans, but rather because of where they were standing.

Dr. Bryant wasn't wearing a professional outfit.

She was here on her private time.

And *in* that time, the single woman had chosen to visit an elderly woman shoved off into the far reaches of some nightmarish nursing home.

Instead of tending to her own life and needs, Dr. Bryant was carving time out of her day to tend to the life of someone who needed the companionship.

Judging by the needles and yarn left on the lumpy couch, which were being used to knit a pink scarf, she'd been here awhile. Judging by the posters on the walls, this wasn't her first visit.

Artemis paused, mouth open. Forester was still ruefully massaging his nose. Briefly, all Artemis wanted to do was turn and run. The same instinct she'd had when recognizing the voice.

But she'd been running away for so long, she could feel it weighing on her. An exhaustion that settled on her shoulders and pressed down like a giant's fist.

She swallowed faintly, hesitantly. She frowned at Dr. Bryant, and then she made a choice.

Not to lie. Not to hedge.

To tell the truth.

And in a way, it felt relieving to be *able* to trust someone *new*. Someone she'd never trusted before. The more she thought about it, the more she realized the only person in the world she *truly* trusted was Jamie Kramer. And, perhaps, the Washingtons.

But other than that?

SHE RUNS AWAY

Artemis had lived her life like an island. Isolated. Even as she thought this, her conscience pricked her, and she glanced at Agent Forester.

Cameron was watching her out of the corner of his eye, his scarred hand still daintily touching at his nose. He raised an eyebrow expectantly.

Something in the way he looked at her. The coy, mischievous, lupine look in his gaze didn't quite go all the way through.

There was also the grief. That pain that she so often glimpsed lingering there, as if held like heat trapped in coals. Unnoticed unless someone reached out and touched.

And then scalding.

She found her cheeks warming as she looked hastily away, stepping towards Dr. Bryant.

The coroner stepped back, shaking her phone book. "Don't you dare!" she exclaimed. One hand was behind her back, the other still holding the yellowed pages. The woman glared at Artemis and said, "I have something behind my back! You'd better go now or I'll show you what it is!"

"Is it a gun?" Forester said conversationally. He held up a hand as if volunteering an answer. "I don't think it's a gun."

Bryant scowled, but then muttered, "I liked you better when you weren't a murderer." Her hand re-emerged, showing a crochet needle clutched tight. The end was blunted.

Artemis remained at a safe distance, wanting to avoid both needle and phone-book, and said, stuttering, "I... I'm going to tell you the truth, Dr. Bryant, and I need you to listen to me. Please, just listen. We're not here to hurt you. We'll leave. I promise."

"Good, go!"

"Wait. Wait—we need to speak with Mrs. Solenger. Then we'll leave."

"Not a chance!" Dr. Bryant said, fiercely, her nose wrinkling. "Donna and I have been friends for thirty years, little girl. You'll touch that sudoku-playing saint over my dead body."

"Hehehe," said Donna, who was scribbling in another number on her pad of puzzles, again seeming oblivious to the whole affair.

"I was framed!" Artemis blurted out. "Framed for murder by someone who my father must've hired. She dressed up like me. Paid Azin Kartov, the chess player, to go along with it. They lured me to an apartment under the pretense of studying for a match. I left, and I thought everything was okay. She surprised him and shot him, and then framed me for the whole thing. Azin put blood on my sweater when I was there. The security footage was of the accomplice, dressed as me, but only showing me from behind. She memorized what I said during the interaction and repeated it back to Azin. It was all carefully planned and meant to blackmail me."

Dr. Bryant just listened, still breathing heavily, her pink sweater rising and falling, and the faint dress-jewelry flashing under the lights like twinkling stars.

She just watched Artemis, attentive and wide-eyed. "The cops say you did it," Bryant said.

"I know."

"The feds say it."

"I know."

"Your *aunt* said it!" Dr. Bryant exclaimed, pointing at Forester. "I couldn't believe it when I heard. God's honest truth, I said to myself.

Not adorable, little Artemis. So I called Shauna. But she thinks you did it, Artemis. Everyone does. I've seen the footage."

"Faked. They used footage of me walking up, but then footage of them remaking the scene *after* I left."

"Why? Why would anyone go to all that trouble?" Dr. Bryant was usually playful and euphemistic when talking, but now her tone was grim and her eyes frightened.

It bothered Artemis that the woman was experiencing fear due to Artemis' presence. But after a bit, Artemis realized it *wasn't* fear of the variety Artemis initially thought.

Dr. Bryant was scared on behalf of someone.

She was worried about Donna, not herself.

Which was why, needle in hand, she brandished the makeshift weapon and phonebook like a knight in shining armor, wielding a sword and shield, facing down some dragon to protect a damsel in distress.

In this case, said damsel was cackling as she scribbled in some new digit, pumping her wizened fist up and down in triumph. "I'll figure this one yet, Katya!"

Dr. Bryant winced at the name. She swallowed faintly, and then as if feeling the name deserved an explanation, she murmured, "That was her daughter," Miracle said softly. "She's already lost so much. Why are you here, Ms. Blythe?"

"Because, they're going to kill Jamie Kramer and his little sister, Sophie. If I don't... don't *do* something."

"Do what?"

"Help them."

"Help them with *what*?" Dr. Bryant said emphatically, her perfectly trimmed eyebrows rising again. There was an inflection in her voice, and Artemis suspected she knew what it meant. Artemis was being given an opportunity.

One chance to tell the truth to the woman across from her.

If Artemis hedged or lied, then Bryant wouldn't listen further.

Again, she knew the stakes were high. She thought of Jamie... the man she'd loved since she'd been five.

She blurted out, "To break my father out of prison. I went to speak with a warden's wife, but she knew who I was. So if I don't solve this case—the one involving the Aristocrat, then... then it's all over. The warden's wife will turn me in. My father will remain behind bars. And within three more days, Jamie and his sister will be killed."

Artemis was breathing heavily when she finished, and she felt a faint prickle tingling along her hands, down her back.

She shifted uncomfortably, her left leg brushing against the lumpy couch. She glanced down to notice a small pack of star stickers—complete with glitter—resting on the couch.

Dr. Bryant hesitated a moment, swallowed, then said, "It all sounds far-fetched."

"I know."

"I shouldn't believe you."

"I know."

"Give me a reason, Artemis," Dr. Bryant said quietly. There was a pleading look in her gaze, as if *begging* Artemis for permission to trust.

Artemis hesitated, winced, then said, "I... I don't mean this to sound threatening. But here's a reason: Forester has a gun. If we had wanted to harm either of you, he would've pulled it by now."

She winced as she said it, having uttered the words quickly, like pulling a band-aid.

She allowed the comment to settle, set between them and left alone.

For a moment, Dr. Bryant glanced at Forester, then back at Artemis. She looked at Cameron, "Glock?" she said simply.

"Nah," he replied. "Got a new sidearm. Went old-fashioned this time."

Dr. Bryant narrowed her gaze. "Wimp," she said.

He chuckled.

But the sound died on his lips as Dr. Bryant dropped her sewing needle, and—in a motion as fast as light—pulled a *much* bigger weapon from where it had been hiding in her waistband, under her sweater. She pointed it directly at Forester, then murmured to Artemis, "I was hoping you'd say that," she said quietly. "Because if he *had* threatened me, I would've put a hole the size of Nebraska in that lovely, muscled chest of his."

Artemis stared at the gun.

Forester swallowed faintly, his Adam's apple bouncing. He said, hesitantly, "I—er... I've seen the evidence. Artemis didn't do it." He winced. "Jamie *is* in trouble."

A long sigh.

Dr. Bryant kept her gun pointed at the two of them. She said, "I should tell you... I still don't know if I believe you. And," she added emphatically, "About two minutes ago, I placed a call to 9-1-1." She pulled briefly at the hem of her sweater, revealing the gleam of a phone tucked in where she'd been hiding her hand earlier.

Artemis blinked and swallowed, staring in alarm at the giant weapon in those dainty, manicured hands. The gun was far larger than Forester's and looked as if the bullets might take a limb off in one shot.

The hand-cannon, maintained in a steady grip, pointed at Forester's head. Dr. Bryant said, quietly, "I wanted to hear it for myself, without this... and..." She winced, sighing in frustration. "Dear Lord help me... I don't know, Artemis." Her expression softened as she glanced at the chess master and winced.

Artemis was stunned to see actual tears in the gun-toting coroner's eyes.

Her voice quavering now, heavy with emotion, Dr. Bryant said, "I want to believe you, dear. I really, really do. And..." She sniffed, glancing at Forester. "I don't know kung-fu. I'm sorry I lied."

Forester swallowed again, forcing a smile that didn't reach his eyes. "Sure... yeah. I forgive you. Now how about we point that thing someplace else?"

"No!" Dr. Bryant snapped. "You mentioned the Aristocrat. That's why you're here? To speak with Donna about her daughter? Well, I refuse. Donna has been a friend of mine forever, and I'm not about to let you trouble her by—"

"The Aristocrat?" said a voice from the bed.

Everyone went quiet. Something in the voice sent goose-pimples up Artemis' spine.

Chapter 13

The three of them standing by the lumpy couch all turned to glance at the woman now sitting upright in the bed. The woman was frowning now, staring at the intruders in her home with a severe expression that only became more pronounced due to the wrinkling of her skin.

She glared at all of them and didn't look away.

Artemis swallowed faintly, shooting a quick look towards Forester then back.

The woman's gaze was clear, her eyes lucid all of a sudden. The math puzzle rested on her desk of blankets, the small orange pencil tucked neatly into the metal-ringed spine of the booklet.

"How do you know that name?" Mrs. Solenger asked.

The woman had to be in her eighties, perhaps even older. Her skin was wrinkled and the creases near her eyes stretched. She glared at them, watchful and silent.

Artemis shifted uncomfortably. She opened her mouth to speak, but Dr. Bryant beat her to it. "It's nothing, Donna. They were just leaving."

But Dr. Bryant scowled in frustration as Artemis stepped forward, raising a hand and calling out in greeting. "Mrs. Solenger? My name is Artemis. I wanted to ask you about your daughter, Katya."

Dr. Bryant was frowning so deeply from behind her sparkling glasses that the furrow in her brow pushed her glasses half an inch lower on her nose. *You go girl* didn't seem like particularly solid footing in that moment, but Artemis couldn't back down.

Not now.

She had to remember what was at stake.

"Katya?" said the old woman, her voice shaking at the word. A faint, misty smile appeared, and the old woman stared across the room, her small hands gripping the hem of her blankets. Her fingers trembled where they pressed, and those frail lips were pressed in a thin line as if attempting to hold back a sudden flood of words.

"Yes, ma'am," said Artemis. In her mind, she had a running clock, attempting to determine how long until the police showed up from Dr. Bryant's call. Fifteen minutes tops. So they had ten, then needed to leave. Ten was plenty. Ten could give them answers. But also... if she didn't get *something*, Jamie and Sophie were dead.

"No, Donna. Ignore them. They're troublemakers. Probably even murderers!" Dr. Bryant said. Then, in a flash of conscience, she winced and added, "Though I'm not a hundred percent on that last part. So... ignore them."

"Murderers..." Mrs. Solenger whispered. She nodded faintly, and the few strands of pale hair on her head shifted as she sat further upright in her cot.

She was staring towards them, but not *quite* seeing, and she leaned forward a bit, narrowing her eyes, suggesting her vision wasn't great at any distances more than a foot.

Her voice had a creaking quality to it, like old hinges or oak cabinets. The woman said, "Katya was murdered. They never found her, you know. Miracle... did I tell you about that night?"

"Yes, Donna. Many times. It's fine. Please... please lay back down."

Dr. Bryant was still aiming her hand-cannon towards the two intruders, but her concern was causing her to glance around and wince in the direction of her bedridden friend.

Donna sighed, letting out a faint exhale. "I like talking about Katya..." she said softly, leaning back all of a sudden again, as if exhausted. "It was nicer back then..."

Artemis felt her heart pang in her chest, but she took another step towards the bed, despite Dr. Bryant's glares and gun.

Artemis didn't think the kindly coroner would shoot her. It was a gamble, at this point, she was willing to take.

"Mrs. Solenger," Artemis said softly, "Can you tell *me* about Katya? Please? I'd love to hear what you know. I'm looking for the man who..." a swallow. "Who *hurt* your daughter."

"Killed her," said Solenger softly, still leaning back against her pillow, the soft fabric indented by the woman's head. "That's what happened. No sense mincing words, dear. My Katya is dead. I knew it the night she vanished. I could feel it in my soul..." A little laugh. "My husband loved our daughter so dearly. He beat me to the reunion.

I intend to join them soon." Mrs. Solenger gave a giggle, and it was almost girlish and didn't feel like a sound that belonged in this place at all.

The giggle turned to a faint cough, which seemed more apropos for the setting. But Solenger said, "Miracle, I've told you how welcome you are, haven't I? One day, in those streets of gold, wherever we live... You're permanently welcome in our home. Always, lovely child."

Dr. Bryant was staring at the bed, smiling faintly, her eyes tear-stained once more. The coroner nodded. "I've always appreciated the invitation to your heavenly mansion, Donna. But you're not there quite yet, my iron lady. Hmm? It's time for bed, isn't it?"

But Solenger ignored this comment, chuckling as she leaned forward again and pointed a wizened and arthritic finger towards Dr. Bryant. In a faint whisper, Donna said to Artemis, "She's a real dear, but she never married. Pity. She's quite good-looking, don't you think, Amos?"

Artemis hesitated, then realized this was directed at her. She coughed delicately, and said, "I... yes. Very lovely."

Dr. Bryant sniffed. "I'm not single from lack of *offers*," she said with an air of wounded pride. "Just from a lack of interest in those offers."

Artemis took the comment to mean that Dr. Bryant wasn't yet in a violent mood, though, she still carried herself with some fear and caution. Another step forward, and Miracle was forced to retreat to keep between Artemis and the bed.

The hand-cannon, though, lowered a bit now, pointing towards the tiled floors. Which, unlike the rest of the building, were pristine, mopped and swept. Artemis wondered if this was Dr. Bryant's doing.

In addition, Artemis didn't know what to think of all this talk about death and reuniting on the other side.

It was a lovely picture. And she would never steal someone's hope, especially since it was in such short supply. But if Artemis was pressed into a corner and asked for her preference, she would far rather find Helen again on *this* side of the six-foot journey.

And there was *another* person she needed to find.

"Can you tell me about the night Katya disappeared?" Artemis said quietly. "Was anything strange? Did she tell you anything odd that week that had happened?"

"Hmm? What's that, Amos? Odd? Yes, yes, *very* odd. Katya didn't come home that night. She always came home."

"She was a rule-follower then," Artemis asked quickly.

"I suppose so, yes. She liked to draw. Sometimes she drew boys she found pretty. She never *could* quite get the eyes right, though. Pity. She could've been very good if she'd been able to study the eyes more." Another faint cough, and it looked as if Mrs. Solenger was losing her strength, but she returned with renewed vigor and said, "In fact, my daughter never could quite meet someone's eyes. Too shy. Bashful."

Artemis hesitated. She could feel her anxiety mounting, and the clock in her mind, tracking the arrival of the cops Dr. Bryant had called, was quickly running out of time. Only a few minutes left. The cops would show up in eight or so. They needed at least five to get away. But again, she severed this anxiety, this fear. The cops didn't know *which* room the call had been placed from, and the nursing home was large. Besides, she simply couldn't leave empty-handed. Not now. Artemis settled in her mind she wouldn't leave. Not until she *had* something to go on. So Artemis continued to press, the urgency plucking the words from her throat, "I... I'm very sorry for your loss. But—"

"No buts," Miracle whispered, "Please... Please, Ms. Blythe. It's time to go."

But Artemis ignored this, even though it irked her to do so. Instead, she said, "Is there anything about that night you remember, Mrs. Solenger."

"Hmm? What night?"

"The night Katya disappeared."

"You knew Katya?"

"No, but I'm sure I would've liked her if I did."

"Yes... yes, everyone loved Katya," said Solenger smiling and letting out a little breath. She closed her eyes now, breathing faintly, her head reclining against the pillow.

Artemis felt her frustration spike but tensed as Dr. Bryant leaned in now. She kept her gun aimed at the floor but was frowning still. "I knew Katya," Dr. Bryant said firmly. "She was about my age when she disappeared."

"Thirty years ago, right?" Forester said. "Katya was the Aristocrat's first victim."

"Nosy," said Dr. Bryant, shaking her head. "Not nice to ask a woman her age, not even with math. Now, listen, Katya was a good girl. She liked to draw, to hike, liked her friends. She didn't have any enemies. She was taken by someone outside. Someone who just wanted to sow chaos..." Dr. Bryant clicked her tongue. "Can either of you think of anyone *else* like that, hmm? Anyone who might be bombarding a dear old lady with inappropriate questions while on the run from the cops? Hmm?"

"Who are you calling old!" came a croaking voice from the bed, though Donna's eyes remained sealed.

Artemis chewed her lip, all too aware of the time running out. Would the cops be here in a few minutes? Would they arrive faster than anticipated?

She said, hurriedly, "No one. I'm not trying to be inappropriate," she said quickly, to Dr. Bryant. "I'm trying to find the man who killed Katya. The same man who, ten years later, killed a young woman by the name of Bella, kidnapping her as well. The Aristocrat has left a trail of bodies in his wake, and he deserves to *stay* behind bars for the rest of his life!"

"Stay?" said Dr. Bryant, frowning. "I wasn't aware they ever arrested anyone."

"I... Oh, did I say stay?" Artemis said hesitantly. "Umm... No, sorry. I just meant." She hesitated, trying to move her mind from her father. But Otto Blythe's face kept appearing in her thoughts, a taunting, grim face.

She scowled and tried to shift to another subject.

But now, Forester's hand rested on her shoulder and he murmured, "We should go." He was glancing at his phone. "Responding units to the 9-1-1 call are only a few minutes away."

Artemis huffed in frustration. They hadn't *learned* anything. They'd already known most of the victims were pretty young women, from good families who had a penchant for drawing or painting. The killer had a type, but it didn't help them find the bastard.

Artemis could feel her pulse quickening, her eyes drawn towards the door.

She turned to Dr. Bryant, and said, "Do you remember anything? Anything at all?"

Miracle hesitated, still tense. "I... The police will be here soon," she said.

Artemis stared. "You do. You know something, don't you?"

"No, I don't," Miracle said firmly, no deception in her tone. "I just remember that night, because I was there. They'd invited me for dinner."

Artemis hesitated. "You were there the night Katya vanished?"

"Yes."

"That's great news!" Artemis exclaimed. Then paused, frowned and said, "I mean... you know what I mean. You can help us remember!" She shot a quick glance towards Donna, not wanting her comment to be thought of as an aspersion. But Artemis said, even more firmly, "Please, Dr. Bryant. I need your help."

"Artemis," Forest said more insistently. "We need to go. *Now*!"

"Dr. Bryant," Artemis said, pleading, "Please. *Please*. We need your help."

"Oh goodness," Miracle whispered. "Oh..." she let out a long breath, wincing. "I... Artemis, I want to believe you. I do. But I saw those videos. I saw—"

Artemis cursed and reached into her pocket. Everyone flinched. But she pulled out a phone.

She stared at Miracle. Forester leaned in, snagging her arm, beginning to pull her towards the door. "Now! Leave now!"

But Artemis yanked her hand free, and exclaimed to Dr. Bryant, "Here! Right here, I can prove it! I was framed. Listen to this!"

And then, Artemis placed a phone call.

She stood in the middle of the nursing home room, refusing to follow Forester back into the hall. He was cursing now, and saying, "Cops are two minutes away, Artemis!"

Dr. Bryant was still shaking her head, looking flustered and confused and sad. One of her feet was tapping rhythmically against the floor, but it wasn't a merry, jovial tap. More like the routine staccato of a funeral march.

But Artemis had made her call.

Jamie's life was on the line. Sophie was going to die.

She had to do *something*. Too many obstacles. Too many failures. No... No, she couldn't leave this room without answers, and Dr. Bryant had *been there* the night of the disappearance.

If anyone could remember, it was the waspishly intelligent coroner.

And if Artemis had to *prove* she was trustworthy, then so be it.

The phone in her hand was vibrating as it attempted to connect. Artemis stared determinedly at Dr. Bryant, holding the phone away from her body as it connected.

Forester eyed the number Artemis had dialed from memory, then gaped, "Shit—what the hell are you doing?"

But Artemis held a finger to her lips suddenly.

The call connected, and then a voice answered. The same voice that had taunted Artemis over the phone only a few days before.

The voice that belonged to the psychotic woman who had kidnapped the Kramers.

A swallow, a chuckle, then Fake Helen said, in a singsong voice, "Well, sister... I was *not* expecting this. I hope you have a *very* good reason for interrupting my manicure." A hesitation. "Or else... Should I add that part? The or else? I felt it was implied." A faint chuckle at her own humor, then, colder, like the sibilant hiss of a snake, "So, what do you want, Artemis?"

CHAPTER 14

Artemis went still, listening to the taunting voice.

The first time Artemis had encountered the woman, she'd been unkempt, dirt-streaked and only recently recovered from one of the Professor's burial coffins.

According to Fake Helen, she'd taken the place of one of the Professor's victims—without the notorious killer having noticed—and lay in wait for Artemis.

This story still wasn't confirmed, and Artemis had her suspicions about the veracity of the tale.

Now, though, as the voice filled the nursing home's room, a low quiet descended over everyone. Eyes glanced back and forth.

Dr. Bryant was frowning, staring at Artemis with a look of suspicion and extreme curiosity.

Forester was staring at his phone and tapping his wrist where he wore a golden, skeleton watch visible just past the sleeve. In fact, she thought it was the same watch he'd worn when they'd first met each other.

She stared at the watch for a moment, cleared her throat, then said, in a low voice, "I need to speak with Jamie."

A crackle of static, suggesting the connection from the woman's burner phone wasn't the best. "Now, now, Artemis—I thought I was clear. You get your handsome squeeze toy back only once *I* get what *I* want."

"Is that it?" Artemis said sharply. "Is Otto..." she swallowed. "*Your* squeeze to—"

"Yuck, sister, really? He's my *dad*. Don't be gross."

"You're not my sister," Artemis said firmly. And she knew it in her bones that she was right. This wasn't Helen. The last time, the woman had known things about Artemis' childhood. Had claimed to remember childhood memories only Helen would've known.

At first, it had terrified Artemis, that somehow *this* psychopath was Helen Blythe.

But then... the story had fallen apart.

For one, the woman hadn't remembered encountering Tommy, their brother, at a waterfall and giving him a note-puzzle. In addition, she'd slipped a couple of times, referring to Helen in the third person.

And finally, she wasn't at all the woman Artemis remembered. Not just in personality—though deranged killer certainly hadn't been Artemis' experience of her older sister.

But more than that.

Helen, the prettier *and* smarter of the two of them according to most people, had been kind, erudite and careful with her words.

SHE RUNS AWAY

The words she used, the vocabulary, the cadence of her speech was *very* different than what this woman on the phone chose to employ. The woman had made mistakes, and Artemis knew her sister. The two of them had been inseparable for *years* until Helen had vanished.

This was someone's idea of a sick joke. Someone was feeding information to Fake Helen, and Artemis had a pretty good idea *who* it was.

Otto Blythe was the one benefiting from all of this, wasn't he? He was the one they were going to help escape from prison.

It made sense that *he* was the one pulling the strings, who had somehow found this strange woman and taught her to play the role of Artemis' best friend and older sister.

But the ruse wouldn't work.

The *real* question was whether *Artemis'* own ruse might work.

"Just let me speak to Jamie," Artemis said cautiously. "I need to know he's okay. It's been days. For all I know, you've killed him."

A pause, then a cold reply, lacking the taunting humor from before. "For all you know, I'll kill him now, sister."

"Stop calling me that."

"Sister? Isn't that what Helen *is* to you?"

"See, you did it again. Helen. You called her in the third person."

"You know what I mean!" the voice snapped, angry and petulant now.

Helen had never been petulant. Always reserved, careful, and *waspishly* clever. This woman... she was erratic, unpredictable and dangerous.

"Please," Artemis said, trying a different tactic. "Let me speak with him."

"Artemis..." the voice said suddenly, and there was a new tenor to it that sent shivers up Artemis' spine.

"What?"

"Why are there police cars approaching your location?"

Artemis froze in place, swallowing, her heart hammering. How did Helen know that? There was no way the woman was keeping track of them, was she?

And this phone... A new number. Artemis had been careful.

She shot a quick look at Forester, then down at his phone. She pointed at it and raised her eyebrows. Forester frowned, glanced at the device, then turned it off instantly.

A second later, the voice on the other line exhaled. "Don't be silly, sister. I already know you're there. Turning it off won't help. And I also know where the fifty cops on patrol in the vicinity should be. One of them just made a beeline towards you. *Why*?"

The final word was cold and demanding, uttered with the cadence and finality of a judge's gavel.

"We... we didn't speak to any cops," Artemis said hurriedly.

"Don't lie to me, sister."

"I'm not!"

Now, there was the sound of heavy breathing, thumping steps, as if the figure on the other line was pacing rapidly back and forth. The woman on the other line was breathing heavily, muttering darkly as she did.

"I thought I could *count* on you Artemis. Just like when we were kids. But now? Now you think I'm stupid. You think to talk to the police. What was the one rule? *Not to talk to cops.* Wasn't it?"

"We're not talking to them," Artemis said hurriedly. "I... I don't know what you want!"

"Prove it. Video feed. Right now!"

"No!"

"Do it!" snapped Helen. "I swear, if you don't, I'll walk downstairs and blow his brains out all over her cute little backpack. Do you hear me, bitch? Do it! Show me where you are. Show me the room. You have ten seconds. Hurry."

Then Helen hung up. Artemis breathed slowly, swallowing, glancing around the room.

"Seven... six... five..." Forester said grimly. At the same time, he was glancing towards the door of the nursing home's room, watching closely.

At any moment, Artemis expected the door to break in. Would the cops know which floor they were on? It was a mercy they hadn't checked in, but Forester had shown his badge, careful to hide his name on it. How closely had the desk attendant been watching?

"Four... three..." Forester began.

Dr. Miracle Bryant dove behind the couch suddenly, flashing a quick thumbs up. Artemis cursed, placed the video call, and raised her phone, glaring into the screen.

A moment. The call paused, struggling to connect over the bad reception, and then a dark screen confronted Artemis. Video denied on the other party's line.

But Artemis' own video was in full view, showing her panicked features. Quickly, she rearranged her expression, breathing slowly.

She'd wanted to speak to the kidnapper not because she was hoping to antagonize. Not even to speak to Jamie. It was so dangerous.

But because the only way forward was to find out what had happened to Katya Solenger, and the only person with a working memory who'd *been* there that night *needed* to know that Artemis wasn't guilty of murder.

The only way she could think of clearing her name had been to introduce the sweet, long-suffering Dr. Miracle Bryant to the wrecking ball of a person that was Fake Helen.

Now, though, the gambit seemed to have paid off.

At least, the way Dr. Bryant had wedged herself under the couch seemed to suggest this.

The bright, pink sweater was visible at the wrong angle, and so Artemis took a quick step forward, her phone directed away.

"Show me the room!" snapped Helen's voice, the dark screen immobile.

"Alright," Artemis said quickly. "Look—see?" She swiveled the phone one way then the other.

"Wait—stop! Who's that idiot?"

"Forester," Artemis snapped back.

"She coulda been talking about anyone," Forester muttered.

"Okay... Right, I remember. The wolf pretending to be a puppy. He follows you around with that pining look in his eyes, doesn't he?"

"Nice to hear from you again, you psychotic bitch," Forester said congenially. "I hope you choke on throat warts."

A chuckle. "Charming as ever."

"Who's that in the corner? I saw her. Show me."

Artemis shifted the phone again, directing it towards the woman who was lying on the bed, resting quietly.

"Just a witness," Artemis said hurriedly. "I have a way into the prison, but I have to solve an old case."

"A what?" the voice perked up in curiosity.

Now that she'd determined the room was clear, and that Artemis and Forester weren't in a police car or being interrogated in some police station, Fake Helen seemed interested again.

"An old case," Artemis said quickly. Then, seeing no harm in it, she added, "The Aristocrat. Know that one?"

"Oh, *him*?" said the voice, sounding excited all of a sudden. A giggle, this one not like a schoolgirl's but more like the bubbling of acid eating through old bones. "He's one of my absolute *favorites*! He was never caught, was he? Operated for twenty-eight years exactly. Eight victims. But there could've been more. His paintings are valued at nearly twelve million dollars. *Each*. That's gone up exponentially in the last two years." The woman rattled the information off with both delight and excitement.

Artemis wrinkled her nose in disgust, unsure *how* this person had all the information on the top of her head. She wondered if the Professor saw himself in competition with other killers. Maybe they had their own little killer club or something.

It gave Artemis the creeps.

She didn't let this creep into her tone, however, as she said, "So... do you know *who* the Aristocrat is? Would make my job much easier."

"No. I don't," Helen said, sounding disappointed. "I'd *love* his autograph. Yes! Let's add that. If you don't get me his autograph, I'll kill Jamie!" She said it cheerfully as if simply requesting a bite from someone's steak at a dinner party.

"Hang on," Artemis said quickly. "That wasn't the deal."

"Oh, relax. I'm joking. Mostly. Though... well... I *really* do want his autograph. He's something of a celebrity in my world."

"Yeah?" Artemis said. "Well... you seem to know a lot about him. If you can help me find out *who* the Aristocrat was and why he stopped his spree, then I can give you the Ghost Killer."

"He has a name, you know. It's *dad.*"

"That isn't his name."

"Same difference. Look, Artemis, are you asking me what I *think* you're asking?"

The voice sounded excited.

"I... I don't know. What do you think I'm asking?"

"Oh—you are, aren't you! No—don't be shy. You want your big sister to help you solve this thing, don't you? You *need* me. Say it, Art. Say that you need me."

"I... could use all the information I can get," Artemis said, biting back the million and one *other,* far less amicable retorts that came to mind.

"Hmm, well *this* is interesting, isn't it? Tell me what we know so far!"

Artemis hesitated, staring at the phone, confusion settling on her like a cloak. She swallowed and shot a quick look towards Forester.

Cameron was frowning, standing at the door and gesturing at his watch again. So far, no one had broken down the door, which meant for the moment, they still had time.

Dr. Bryant's back, clad in that vibrant-hued sweater, was still visible out of the coroner of Artemis' eye from where the coroner had tucked herself to avoid being seen in the room.

"We don't know much," Artemis said softly. "I've only just started looking."

"The warden's wife? That's the play, isn't it?" said Fake Helen, delighted. "I wasn't sure *how* you were going to tackle this, but the warden's wife is as good a bet as any. Hell, I think I might've made the same call."

Artemis hesitated, and then she frowned, feeling a cold shiver along her spine. The woman was clever—that much was clear. She was resourceful.

But *who* was she?

The question kept nipping at Artemis' mind, but now wasn't the time to go digging.

She approached the door now, and Forester was peering out into the hall, through the peephole. He grimaced, pointed and held up two fingers, wincing.

Artemis tensed, listening through the metal door to the sound of knocking, then voices. By the sound of things, the cops were doing the rounds with the other denizens on this floor.

Time was most assuredly not on their side.

Artemis said, "I need to know Jamie and Sophie are alive. That's all the help I want from you."

"Well you're no fun," replied the woman. She sighed, but then muttered, "I guess fine. If you find it *motivating*. And seeing as you're not in a police station. Turn the phone again, just so I can see the door."

Artemis complied.

The woman said, "Just so we're clear, I have eyes and ears everywhere. If you're talking to the cops, you know the cost." Then, before

Artemis could retort, the woman called out, her voice quieter all of a sudden, suggesting she'd lowered her receiver. "Stay back from the door, handsome, I'm coming in."

Artemis tensed, listening to the sound of footsteps. Then a faint *clack* of metal against metal. Artemis hesitated, wondering if a door handle had been turned, or if the phone was now tapped against something solid.

A pause, then a faint rattling sound.

Artemis couldn't quite track the noises, but a second later, she heard a familiar sound.

A voice that sent a quiver through her chest.

"Please... please, Sophie is thirsty. We need water! Hey—hey, I'm talking to you!" The voice was suddenly cut off with a loud clanging sound.

A second later, Fake Helen's voice returned. "There you have it. Prince Charming just *waiting* for his rescue. Now, damsel dearest, stop wasting my damn time and bring me what I want."

Then, the phone clicked off.

Artemis stood quiet, motionless in the room, allowing her heart to calm from where it was pounding wildly. She shot a quick look towards Forester, who was standing grimly by the door, watching her.

He winced and shrugged apologetically. Artemis felt that same quiver from before in her chest, threatening to constrict. Could feel her stomach wanting to tumble to her toes. She let out a shaking little breath, feeling goosebumps forming along her arms.

"That was him," she said grimly, swallowing once. In the background, desperate. It broke her heart to hear him like that. So close and yet so far...

A small, niggling portion of her mind wondered what might happen if she *couldn't* figure out how to solve this. If she couldn't bring the kidnapper what was demanded.

And even if she did, there were no guarantees Fake Helen would release Jamie.

Artemis stood there, trembling, feeling her chest tighten.

And then a loud knock on the door.

Two quick thumps of a pounding fist, and then a deep voice. "Police! Open up please, routine wellness check!"

Chapter 15

As the pounding fist on the door subsided, Artemis tensed. Forester stared at her, mouth open. They both glanced sharply towards Dr. Bryant. Now that the phone call was over, the coroner had been wriggling out from where she'd hidden behind the couch, and she rose to her feet, adjusting her sleeves and breathing heavily. A few strands of her dyed hair were out of place, which she neatly adjusted with a huff.

She then turned her attention to the door, frowned, and shoved her hand-cannon back into her waistband, hiding it under her sweater.

She primped a bit, smoothing her hair, and then a smile appeared on her lips. Artemis hadn't noticed at first, but the woman's lipstick had a green tinge.

Dr. Bryant shot both of them a quick look. She hesitated only briefly and then sidestepped Artemis, moving towards the door.

More pounding. "Open up, police!"

Forester stepped in as if to intercept Dr. Bryant, but the coroner elbowed him out of the way, and Artemis gave Forester a quick shake of her head.

The gambit had been to use the phone call in order to show Dr. Bryant she *wasn't* lying. Fake Helen hadn't exactly been subtle about her role in all of this.

Now, Dr. Bryant reached the door.

The coroner frowned briefly, glanced back, and then her eyebrows went up as she made a shooing motion with her hand.

Forester and Artemis both quickly stepped aside. Neither of them went behind the couch, but they moved out of line of sight from the door.

Dr. Bryant sighed slowly, looked at Artemis and held her gaze for a moment. Something passed between the two women.

Miracle looked resigned, as if she'd made up her mind but was fearful she might regret it. The look she gave Artemis made it all too clear whose fault it would be if it turned out Artemis had been lying this whole time.

Artemis nodded once in what she hoped was an encouraging look.

Dr. Bryant's expression softened only briefly, and her eyes were tender once more. She murmured something that Artemis couldn't quite hear across the room, but by reading lips, she discern the phrase, "*You poor dear.*"

And then Dr. Bryant opened the door.

Not wide, just enough to peer through the crack.

"Hello?" said a deep voice from in the hall. "Who are you?"

"Dr. Miracle Bryant," the woman said cheerfully, smiling with those green-tinted lips. "And what a pleasure it is to meet you, officer.

What's your name? I like your mustache by the way. No beard. It's a bold statement." Miracle flashed a thumbs up.

The officer paused, hidden by the doorway, but judging by his silence, clearly taken off guard by this spiel. He gave Miracle a long look, scratched at his chin, then muttered. "Dr. Bryant, do you work here?"

"She doesn't," said another voice from the hall. "But I know her. She's a friend of the patient here. A Mrs. Singleberry."

"Solenger," Dr. Bryant corrected calmly.

"Yes, yes. Dana Singleberry," said the voice.

This time, Dr. Bryant made no effort to correct the person.

The booming voice, which Artemis gauged to be that of the officer, changed now. A bit more polite. A bit less demanding. "Well, Dr. Bryant, we're making routine checks. A phone call was placed from this address."

"Oh?" Dr. Bryant asked calmly. "An unlisted number?"

"I—yes. How did you know that?"

"I'm a coroner, darling. It's my job to know at least *something* y'all do." Another sweet smile.

"Is anyone in there with you, Dr. Bryant?"

Forester and Artemis both tensed where they'd pressed against the wall at the end of the hall, beneath the poster of *Jesus Shaves*.

They both listened intently, both breathing heavily.

A second passed, and then Dr. Bryant said, "I haven't seen anyone besides Donna, and she's sleeping."

"Donna... that's Mrs. Singleberry?"

"Yes."

"Well... if you see anyone, please let us know. What's the number for your phone, by the way, Ms. Bryant?"

Dr. Bryant didn't correct the misused prefix. Instead, she just smiled again, her hand reached through the door, and it sounded as if she were patting someone on the forearm. "Bless your heart," she said. "You'd have to buy me at least two drinks before asking a lady for her number—don't you know that officer?"

A few muttered comments met this teasing, but then the sound of footsteps and fading voices suggested the figures in the hall were moving away from the door.

Dr. Bryant waited a few moments, then shut the door behind her with a *click,* before locking it again.

And then she turned, her back pressed to the doorframe, her cheerful expression fading all of a sudden. She stared at Forester and Artemis with a look of horror in her eyes.

"You poor thing," she whispered, staring at Artemis. "It's true, then. That horrible, horrible woman on the phone. She really has Mr. Kramer and his daughter?"

"It's his sister, but yeah."

"And you can't go to the police?"

"They suspect me of murdering a federal and a chess player," said Artemis quietly. "That woman on the phone mentioned she'd give evidence that clears my name if I do what she wants."

"Which is what, exactly?"

Forester shot Artemis a sidelong look, which she swiftly ignored, stepping forward instead and facing Dr. Bryant.

"We need to find the Aristocrat," Artemis said simply.

"On the phone... she said... are you really going to break the Ghost-killer out of prison?" Dr. Bryant said quietly. She hesitated, bit her lip, then said, "Oh my... I'm involved now, aren't I?" She hesitated briefly, looking troubled for only a split-second before her eyes widened and her mouth formed a small circle. "I'm going to be the best murder accomplice you've *ever* seen, Artemis Blythe! Just you watch!" She leaned in, giving Artemis a quick hug.

The coroner smelled of peach sherbet and dill relish. A strange combination but, knowing the woman, most likely an intentional one.

"Do you like that?" Dr. Bryant said suddenly, noticing the way Artemis had inhaled through her nose. "I make it myself. Would you like a bottle?"

"Umm, sure. Maybe later," Artemis said quickly. "It smells lovely. But please, I don't need an accomplice, ma'am."

Dr. Bryant wrinkled her nose.

"I mean, *Miracle,*" Artemis said quickly. "I need to know what happened that night."

Dr. Bryant didn't ask for clarification about *what* night. They all knew. Mrs. Solenger on the bed was breathing softly, eyes closed. Artemis couldn't tell if she was listening. A part of her hoped not.

She didn't want to make the mother of the Aristocrat's first victim live through that horrible night all over again.

Dr. Bryant, of a similar sentiment, spoke softly, frowning as she did. It was a testament to the woman's loyalty that once she'd decided Artemis was in the clear, no guile, no suspicion remained in her gaze. She stood close, as a confidant, and spoke quickly.

"I can tell you what I remember," she said.

"If I recall," Artemis replied, "You have a very good memory."

"Well, thank you, sweetheart. I'd like to think so. But you're going to have to help me. Most of the questions I answer involve the dead. I don't know what you're looking for."

"Tell me about the night Katya disappeared," Artemis replied quickly. "What do you remember?"

"I was invited over for dinner. My parents were out of town, and different families in the church had agreed to help feed me and my siblings. My brother was at a friend's house, and so I went to the Solengers." She glanced over to the bed, a wafer-thin smile affixed to her face. Her gaze held a distant quality.

She continued, "Pecan-glazed meatloaf and mashed potatoes with balsamic sauce. I can still smell it if I think hard enough."

"And Katya... she was there that night?"

"To start, yes. She was about my age. Both of us having just turned twenty, I believe. Those were the days... You should have seen me. All the men wanted my number then." She gave a forlorn little sigh. "I had options," she added more adamantly, likely remembering Mrs. Solenger's comments from earlier.

"Of course. I don't doubt it for a minute. But Katya was there?"

"Yes, but she got a phone call and had to leave halfway through the meal."

"She did? Who called? What time?"

"I..." Dr. Bryant hesitated, closed her eyes. Then shook her head. "I didn't see the clock. I don't know. About the time they were serving apple cobbler and vanilla bean ice cream."

"So after dinner, Katya got a call and then left?"

"Mhmm."

"And her parents... did they think anything was untoward?"

"I don't believe so. Katya was on the debate team, in a painter's club, and she also was on the soccer team. She was often coming and going. She was an introvert, but everyone liked her."

"So you've all said." Artemis hesitated, shifting uncomfortably and rubbing absentmindedly at her sleeve which she gripped between thumb and forefinger.

She glanced towards the bed, then back. "This phone call," she said suddenly. "You don't know who it was from?"

"Not a clue. She didn't say."

"Did she seem *happy* when she received the call?"

"Umm... Yes. Perhaps. She wasn't *unhappy.*"

Artemis said suddenly, "Did she leave *before* eating any dessert?"

"I... yes, she did. Is that relevant?"

"Mrs. Solenger," Artemis called out suddenly.

The woman yawned but opened her eyes to glance over, blinking a few times owlishly.

"I'm very sorry for bothering you, Mrs. Solenger, but this is important. Did your daughter like apple cobbler?"

"Katya? It was her favorite. Did you know Katya?"

Artemis shook her head, forcing a quick, sad smile. But her heart was pounding now. She began to move towards the door, gesturing at Forester to follow.

"What is it?" Dr. Bryant asked quickly. "What's the matter?"

"Whoever called her must've been involved," Artemis said, as she paused by the door, breathing heavily, her skin tingling. "And Katya *liked* cobbler but didn't stay for any."

"So?" Dr. Bryant asked, bemused. "Does that matter?"

"Yes. *Very* much so."

"How?"

"Because," Artemis insisted, closing her eyes briefly and placing herself there that night. Sitting at the dinner table, surrounded by her parents and a childhood friend.

Her brow furrowed and twitched, and she said, quietly, "Did Katya look excited or worried?"

Dr. Bryant hesitated. "I... It was *very* long ago, Ms. Blythe. I very much admire the mind of a chess master, but my recollection isn't nearly as sophisticated, dear."

Artemis glanced over and shook her head. "I don't believe that," she said simply. "You're usually the smartest person in the room, aren't you?"

Dr. Bryant smiled. She winked. "Usually? As in, with *you* here, I'm not."

Artemis blushed, quickly shaking her head. "N-no, that's not what I meant. I'm so sorry!"

"She meant me," Forester chimed in.

Dr. Bryant snickered, briefly snorting with laughter without looking ashamed about the unbecoming sound for an instant. She then tilted her head, sighed heavily and closed her eyes. She waited briefly, as if listening to some distant noise. Then, eyes still closed, long paste-on eyelashes fluttering below eye-shadow speckled with faint grains of glitter, she said, "Both. Excited and worried."

"It had to have been a boy, then," Artemis said quickly. "A man, whatever."

"No," said Bryant firmly.

"It must have been," Artemis replied. "What else would get someone to abandon their favorite dessert looking both worried and excited?"

"Not a boy," said Dr. Bryant. "And no, not what you're thinking either, Cameron. Not a girl."

Forester looked mildly disappointed.

Dr. Bryant shook her head. "Katya was dating someone at the time. A young man—a nice man—by the name of Travis Armonai. The two of them had been dating for a few years by then. She loved him and *never* would have cheated."

"Well," Forester interjected, "then maybe it was this Travis fellow."

"No," Artemis said softly. "After a few years, the emotions change. Excitement, perhaps. But the nerves of anticipation? Not with that level of familiarity."

"Unless she thought he was going to propose," Forester cut in. "Or any number of things."

But Dr. Bryant was shaking her head. "Travis wasn't ready to propose. He was a year younger than her, still figuring things out. No. It wasn't a boy. I would've known. She would've told me."

"Then what?" Forester asked. He hesitated, "I mean... maybe she was just watching her weight, you know. Maybe that's why she skipped the dessert."

Artemis frowned. "But it was from a call that made her look nervous and excited. Anticipation of some sort. Why? What else was she..." Artemis trailed off, thinking, cycling through all the options. There were any number of reports that might have come in to alarm an individual.

But medical news wouldn't have enjoined excitement. Hanging out with friends wouldn't have caused a loss of appetite.

It was difficult. All of this conjecture over an evening from years ago.

But Artemis was a student of human nature. And if the information she was provided was correct, she felt as if she could narrow it all down.

She leaned back, exhaling slowly, thinking through what she'd been told. Part of her mind was distracted by the knowledge that cops were still in the building, searching for them. But she forced her mind to quiet, refusing to linger on the anxiety.

Fear muddied the mind. Artemis exhaled slowly, counting in her head, using a breathing exercise taught to her by one of the shrinks who'd gone through the revolving door of experts who'd attempted to help her over the years.

"A pretty girl," Artemis said softly. "Well-liked. Involved in acti vities... sports... The Aristocrat was a painter and used the blood of his victims too..." She paused and then glanced sharply at Dr. Bryant. "Two questions."

"Alright. Oh my, your tone gave me shivers right there. No, sorry, never mind. Ignore me. What are the questions?"

"Guesses, really. Had Katya applied to college? Some university she wanted to get into?"

"I... I don't believe so. She was going to community college at the time. She seemed quite happy to stay in town."

"Second question, then. What about art competitions? Anything like that?" Artemis was nodding as she said it. The thought fit. People were often most excited about *love, fear* or dreams. In this case, love was ruled out by Dr. Bryant's testimony. Fear was ruled out by the excitement Katya had exhibited.

But dreams?

Everyone had dreams. Things they wanted more than anything in life. Deep, *deep* desires of the heart.

The sorts of things that might conjure both fear and excitement—anticipation. Nervousness...

And the Aristocrat had specifically targeted young women involved in the arts.

Dr. Bryant paused, shaking her head. "Not... not that I can think of."

"The local art exhibit down by the riverwalk," said Donna from the bed.

All eyes darted to her suddenly.

"Excuse me?" said Artemis.

The old woman blinked. "What?"

"What did you just say, ma'am?"

"Do I know you?"

"You mentioned an art exhibit," Artemis said quickly.

But Donna Solenger had returned her attention to her math puzzle again and was shaking her head briefly, murmuring to herself as she entered in a new set of numbers.

Miracle, though, clicked her fingers. "Wait! I remember now. Yes—yes, there was an art exhibit hosted by a museum coming through town. I believe it had some competition too... Judges determining the quality of art, and then choosing one piece in particular to be auctioned. I remember because Katya talked about it for weeks leading up to the date..."

"Maybe she was waiting to hear back," Forester said.

Artemis was shifting back and forth now in excitement. "What was the name of the art exhibit?"

Dr. Bryant shook her head. "That I don't remember, but you'll probably be able to find it online. The Pinelake Gazette did a piece on it, and most of their articles are uploaded online. I sometimes go back through just to remember how things once were..."

Artemis exhaled slowly but then nodded. She shot a look at Forester, who flashed her a thumbs-up.

"Gonna have to make sure they're not waiting for us in the lobby," he said, "But are you good to go?"

"Yeah... yeah, I'm good." Artemis swallowed. "We need to find who was involved in this art competition."

"And *if* Katya submitted anything," Forester said. "It's still conjecture."

"It isn't," Artemis insisted. "It's likelihood. The Aristocrat was a painter, Forester. And Katya received news about her dreams. It fits."

"Because you want it to fit..." Forester hesitated. "Or because you're psychic."

"Ooh, you're a psychic?" said Dr. Bryant.

"Yes," Forester said.

"No! Stop telling people that. Thank you, Dr. Bryant. We need to go. Thank you, Mrs. Solenger!"

"Hmm? Next weekend, young lady."

Artemis didn't know what this meant, but she gave a little wave towards the old woman in the bed who'd lost everything. And yet, there, leaning back, working on her sudoku puzzle, in that cramped, small space, she looked content. Happy even.

And Artemis guessed, in no small part, the effect was caused by Dr. Bryant's presence. The posters on the wall. The aura the woman brought with her wherever she went.

Now, Forester and Artemis were moving towards the door.

Cameron opened it a crack, peering into the hall, then gave a quick nod. Artemis, meanwhile, was fumbling with her phone, already cycling to the Pinelake news sources, filtering them by date and looking up the art exhibit that had come through town thirty years ago.

Chapter 16

One stairwell, a janitor's closet, and two fire escapes later, Forester and Artemis had managed to avoid the beat cops searching the nursing home.

And now Artemis was scanning through the pictures in the old news article from the Gazette. They were moving through the meandering roads at the foot of the Cascade mountains, heading hastily away from Pinelake through swirling mist and terrain lush with green trees dripping with moisture from a morning rain.

The gray clouds above threatened to add downpour to the churning breeze but had yet to release their pent-up burdens.

"I found it," she said hurriedly. "And listen to this... Katya Solenger. Submission number seven. She was going to be in the competition—judged by four professional painters."

Forester, who was driving, shot her a quick look. "Painters?"

"Exactly!" Artemis said, excitement rising. She scanned through the information. "The painters were supposed to interview the competition submissions one at a time."

"One-on-one?" Forester said, quickly.

"Yes! And... Forester, holy shit!" Artemis yelled.

Forester jerked the steering wheel reactively, cursing and leaving rubber on the dark, gray road behind them with a squeal. "What the hell?" he shouted.

"Guess what I found?" Artemis said, still cycling hastily through the news articles. This time, though, she'd advanced to the *next* year of the competition. This time, the museum had hosted it in Northern California.

As Forester slowed, taking the winding roads through the mist at his own pace, he gave a quick shake of his head. "No clue. What?"

"Know the name Laura Heard?"

"No, should I?"

"That was the Aristocrat's second victim."

"And?"

"Guess who won the art competition at the *next* year's exhibit? The year *after* Katya went missing?"

Forester looked straight at her now, strange shadows cast over his face by the way the mist interrupted the light, streaming over the windshield. "You're kidding? Laura Heard *also* submitted something to this thing?"

"Yeah. It goes by different names based on the locality, but the museum in question is based out of Oxford."

"What's the museum called?"

"It... it isn't around anymore, but it looks like the company that ran the museum and the art competitions was called the Chernow Company."

Forester drummed his fingers against the steering wheel, and they swerved again as he ignored the *Slow Speed* sign at a particularly sharp switchback and continued to veer around the bend. The car jolted as they ran over a toppled branch, and Artemis cursed, shaking her head.

"How much further?" she asked.

"To that art judge's house? Five minutes."

Artemis nodded, glancing back down at the article. The contestants' names weren't the only ones listed. The four judges employed by the traveling exhibit were also listed.

"How have we narrowed down to... what was it... Jameson Faber?" Forester shot a look at Artemis.

"Mr. Faber is the only potential suspect left," Artemis replied quietly.

"And why's that?"

"Two of the judges were women."

"Couldn't the killer be a woman?"

"Could be, but unlikely. Both of them were married at the time, with children. To kidnap young women and keep them for days, if not weeks, it would take privacy, seclusion. Also, statistically speaking, women are the *least* likely culprits."

"So we're crossing them out based on statistics?"

"That, and also Veronica Wrought moved back to England after two years, and Amy Edison was battling cancer for two of the years the Aristocrat was active."

"Hmm. Okay then. And so what about the other judge?"

"Emerson Daily," Artemis said, cycling back to the relevant news article. "He died in a car crash eight years before the Aristocrat disappeared. Also off the list."

"So of the four judges, that leaves us with Jameson Faber."

"Exactly."

Artemis read from a social media profile, "Seventy-six years old, lives alone, a professional painter. And get this... he uses some of the same techniques that the Aristocrat does in *his* artwork."

Forester frowned. "So how come the cops never interviewed him?"

"They might not have known the art competition connection," Artemis replied with a shrug. "Plus, Mr. Faber is in a wheelchair."

"Huh. You don't think maybe that rules him out as our guy?"

"I don't know. But I'd like to speak with him either way. Besides, he lives close enough, what could it hurt?"

The GPS chirped as if chiming in with her words. Forester took the next turn, onto a small street marked *Grandma's Lane*.

As they moved along the untended, cracked asphalt road, slowing to avoid potholes, Forester said, "What I don't get... why did this killer, this Aristocrat, disappear? What made him stop?"

"I don't know."

"And why didn't he release his final painting. The one Bella Doler would've inspired."

"Yuck. Inspired. I hate that word for this. But I guess you're right. I don't know that either."

Cameron shook his head, brow furrowed, sighing in frustration.

They followed the GPS down the small road, moving past single-family homes oriented between large trees and behind overgrowth. This cul-de-sac seemed far more interested in privacy, sheltering from the neighbors' prying eyes than it did in uniform displays of well-kept lawns and painted fences.

There *were* fences, but they were not of the white picket variety; rather, these fences were large, only further adding to the apparent desire to keep out prying eyes.

Forester came to a rolling stop. Gravel crunched under their tires, and their vehicle leaned off the side of the road, over the asphalt, onto the dust. The two of them were staring towards the house that the GPS had led them to.

"Well that's not creepy," Forester said quietly.

Both of them were staring at a home that looked to be two hundred years old. Dark, weathered boards crossed over the windows. The front of the house was in ill repair. Two of the steps leading up to the door were missing. Cobwebs under the banister, and mold along the roof, starting at the gutter but spreading out over wooden pieces that had been used to replace old shingles.

Grass had overgrown at the base of the house and stood at least knee height.

Artemis and Forester frowned, staring at the place.

"Think he still lives here?" Forester asked.

"I was wondering something else," she shot back.

"What's that?"

"Why isn't there a ramp?"

"Ha. Good point. If this guy is wheelchair-bound, why the steps? He must not live here."

Artemis hesitated but then said, "Second floor. See?"

They both found themselves staring at a glowing light pulsing from the window.

And then a shadow moved across the glass and paused as if staring out into the street. The dark form behind the smudged glass froze, and Artemis stiffened in her seat. She was confident, behind her tinted windows, that the figure couldn't see her. And yet a trembling shiver crept up her spine.

And then, the figure in the window moved away. The blinds were closed a second later, and the glowing light was turned off.

"Changed my mind. The place is creepy," Forester said conversationally.

She just stared, swallowing slowly, and watching.

The two of them shared a look, and then pushed out of the car.

Forester led the way, up the cracked and fissured driveway, towards the front steps. They avoided the missing stairs, dodging splinters, and the railing itself seemed ready to give out under Forester's grip. They reached the front door though, without event. A sign on the door, weathered like the rest of the house, declared, *No solicitors*. Another sign, below this one, said, *We don't call the police*. And there was a picture of a rifle beneath the words.

Artemis glanced towards a few holes in the door and wondered if they were caused by bullets.

She hoped they were termites. And *then* hoped she would never have to think that way again.

What sort of person desired the presence of termites?

Artemis stepped forward, carefully stepping over the least welcoming welcome mat she'd seen in her life. The black mold alone should've been warning enough. She knocked on the door, half expecting the wood to give way under her fist. But it was solid enough.

Forester reached out and pressed a small button by the door. But the bell didn't ring.

The two of them waited, standing on the moldy doormat.

No response.

Artemis frowned, tried again and called out, "Mr. Faber? We need to speak with you, sir!"

"FBI!" Forester added.

Artemis winced. She wasn't sure *why*, but it seemed somehow wrong to invoke the name of the very people hunting her. She waited, listening.

Still no reply. Behind her, from the street, she heard the sound of trundling tires and glanced back sharply, feeling a jolt of nerves.

A black car with dark windows was slowly rolling past their parked vehicle. She stared at it.

The car didn't stop but kept going, disappearing down the end of the street.

"You're just being paranoid," she whispered to herself, swallowing and nodding. "Just paranoid."

She knocked harder this time. Forester joined in, pounding his fist against the door in the same way the cops had back in Mrs. Solenger's nursing home.

"FBI! Open up!" Forester said, his hand resting on his hip, near his holstered weapon.

And then, suddenly, the door swung open.

Artemis opened her mouth to speak but the words died on her lips. She froze in place, staring at the barrel of the shotgun pointed directly at them.

"Would you quit it with all that damn hollering?" an old, croaking voice snapped.

A man was sitting in a wheelchair, his face wrinkled and drooping, his hands covered in liver spots. He wore a fisherman's hat with fly-fishing hooks tucked in the brim, and he also wore no shirt, indifferent to his flabby, saggy abdomen on full display.

Over his left pectoral, the man had a large tattoo of an anchor.

Inside, the home was in a somewhat better state than its outside. The scent of acrylic paints and glue lingered heavily on the air, and past the man with the fisherman's hat, Artemis spotted a small art studio, visible behind a door of glass.

But she didn't stare towards this studio long. Rather, her attention was captured by the double barrel of the man's brandished weapon.

Forester's own hand lingered on his holster. He swallowed, faintly, eyes narrowing. "Mr. Faber," Forester said slowly, "I'm going to reach for my badge now. Lower that gun, please."

Jameson Faber glared at the two of them and said, "What the hell are you doing pounding on my door? I was working! You bastards cost me half a day's focus. Do you know how damn long it takes to get in flow? Huh? At my age? Pissing every half hour. God dammit. Now get lost!"

He slammed the door in their faces.

Forester blinked. Artemis found she was able to breathe a bit easier, but just in case, she stepped to the side, away from the door.

Forester tried the doorknob, and it opened. He pulled the door slowly open, and the two of them were staring towards the art studio, where the man in the wheelchair was attempting, with limited success, to maneuver through the opening.

At the sound of creaking hinges, though, he glanced back, cursing. "What the hell? Get out of my house, you hooligans!"

Artemis stayed on the porch. Forester stepped into the eccentric artist's home, snatched the shotgun from where it was resting across the man's wheelchair arms, and tossed it onto a couch, away from them.

"Hey! Hey, you oaf—that's mine!"

The shirtless, wizened old man tried to slap at Forester but missed and nearly toppled from his wheelchair. As the thing began to fall, Forester caught it, placing it carefully back upright.

The old man was now turning his chair, muttering darkly as he bumped against Forester's foot a couple of times. Finally, he managed to rotate completely in order to level his glare on the lot of them.

"Assholes!" he snapped.

Artemis sighed. Forester was gesturing at her to join them.

She paused only briefly, glancing back over her shoulder as the dark vehicle trundled past once more, slower this time. She frowned, staring at the car. She couldn't make out the driver through the tinted glass.

She reached out and shut the door firmly behind them and then turned to face the painter.

CHAPTER 17

The man in the wheelchair stared at the two of them, frozen in his seat now, his crooked, liver-spotted fingers tense against the armrests.

His eyes had widened to almost comical proportions, glancing back and forth between the two of them as he exhaled shakily.

"I don't got shit," he said slowly. "Broke as ass."

His Adam's apple bounced, pronounced as he swallowed.

Artemis shook her head, still standing with her back to the door. A slow itch crawled along her spine, and she glanced through a small gap in the boarded-up, lower-level windows to see if she could spot the car with the tinted windows.

But the street was clear again.

She returned her focus to Mr. Faber. The man was leaning back now, as if trying to distance himself from the two intruders with his posture. If he'd heard Forester's calls of *FBI,* he gave no indication that it put him at ease.

The fishhook tassels tucked in the band around his hat shifted as he leaned back and studied them. His bare chest and lumpy belly wobbled from the motion.

Now that she stood closer, Artemis spotted the occasional streak of paint along his body. A smudge of yellow there, a dash of brown here. She then spotted the man's shirt, draped over a chair outside the painting studio.

By the look of things, he'd removed it to avoid getting it soiled.

"Why don't you just use an apron?" Artemis said, quizzically.

"Why don't you just go straight to hell?"

Artemis frowned. Forester grinned. "I like this guy," Forester said.

"Bite me, sasquatch."

Forester hesitated for a second, then, in a cold, shrewd voice he murmured, "You know... we've got you figured out, Faber."

"What? How the hell do you know my name, stretch?"

"Told ya. FBI."

"FBI? Shit. I thought you were advertisers or something."

"I announced myself twice," Forester shot back.

"Yeah, well, hearing ain't what it once was. So what do you think you've got figured? You're interrupting my flow-zone."

"Yuck," Forester said. "You can keep your flow-zone to yourself. We're here to ask you about Katya Solenger and Laura Heard."

"Damn..." He winced. "Alright, you got me. So I like to have some fun." He held up his hands, showing more flecks of paint dried around the knuckles.

Artemis blinked in surprise. "So you admit it?"

"I mean... whatever. Is it a fine? Hang on—not jail time is it? Cuz in that case, those two whores are dirty liars. I never did see 'em. Didn't pay 'em. And they never modeled neither."

The old man rattled this all off with a severe scowl.

Forester and Artemis shared a look. Artemis said, slowly, "Er... sir, who do you think we're talking about?"

"Katya and Laura... That's what you said, right? I mean... Those aren't the names they use in the classifieds, but," he wiggled his white eyebrows which jutted every which way. "I ain't one to ask. You know what I mean?" He gave a randy little chuckle, winking at Artemis.

"Sir," she said coldly, "Please don't wink at me."

"Oh, I get it," Forester said suddenly. "You think we're busting you about a couple of hookers."

"What?" he pressed his stained fingers against his chest and released a mock gasp. "I—I *never*. Hookers? No! How *dare* you. Those are fine art models, good *sir*! So what is it, a fine or jail time?"

"Why would it be either," Forester said, "if they're just fine art models?"

"Ah, shit. Things happen. You know how it is. Couple of horny foxes like them? Stud like myself? Hehehe." Another giggle. He winked at Artemis again.

Artemis sighed. "Sir... you *do* recognize those names, don't you? They're not prostitutes. Katya Solenger and Laura Heard. What about Bella Doler?"

"Huh? Three? I don't remember three... When was this? Couple a weeks ago, right? They posed for me. I paid 'em. It was all kosher. Did they say something else?" Suddenly he went pale, mouth unhinged.

"Wait. Hang on. No-no-no. They're the ones who propositioned *me*! Not the other way around. Those harlots are lying!"

Forester was beaming now, as if he found the whole exchange amusing.

Artemis was massaging the bridge of her nose, attempting to stave off what felt like an inevitable headache. She said, quietly, "Sir... What is it you think we're asking you about?"

"Those girls from two weeks ago. I sometimes hire other ones. I figured they were a bit too hot for this business. Now I get it. They're using the law to try and steal my art. That's it, isn't it? They got really pissy when I refused to give 'em the portrait."

"We're not asking about that," Artemis said firmly. She watched the man, eyes narrowed, wondering if he was just playing the fool or if the role came naturally.

A fly-fishing hook with red feathering shifted in his hat as he turned to look at her. The three-pronged hook dangled from a safety pin and swished across the brim of his round, fisherman's hat.

"What are you going on about, then? Say... are you two really cops? You don't *look* like cops."

"We are," Forester said quickly. He flashed his badge.

"Lemme see the number," the man in the wheelchair said, leaning in.

But Artemis cleared her throat. "Excuse me," she said, firmly, "I'm going to have to ask you, sir—*focus*. We're asking about thirty years ago. The art competitions you judged for. *Chernow Company*. Do you remember?"

At this, he tensed, swallowed faintly, then glanced over at her.

He was frowning now, his eyes cast in shadow for a brief moment. He stared, inhaling shakily, and then holding the breath.

"Now... why do you wanna know about Chernow?" he murmured.

"So you do remember?" Artemis said, feeling a slow tingle spreading along her arms. "And what about Katya? Laura?"

"I don't remember those names," he said. "But I know Chernow. I worked as a judge in one of their competition circuits for a while. Paid well. Good exposure." He just watched her now. "What's this about?"

"The tournament entrants," Artemis said, cautiously. "Did you ever have a chance to speak with any of them one-on-one?"

She wasn't sure the best way to approach this. They weren't coming with hard evidence, but conjecture. In fact, speaking with this man, she wasn't sure if he was just playing them. He seemed completely out of it. Silly and frail—not like some heinous kidnapper and killer who had tortured young women and used their blood in trophies.

And yet there he sat in that chair of his, swallowing faintly, and looking nervous all of a sudden.

"What... what about it?" he said slowly. "I mean... well, one on one? Nah. Nah, nothing like that. Who said that?"

Artemis paused. Then tried a lie. "You were seen, sir. We have a witness saying you spoke to Katya Solenger alone. The night she disappeared."

At this last word, his face went as pale as a sheet. His hands gripped his arm rests as tightly as she thought his fingers might manage without popping a knuckle.

He swung his head adamantly back and forth, and practically yelled, "They're a damn liar! Whoever said that shit. They're lying! I never did that. Never spoke to no one. Not a single one."

"Aw, come on now," Forester said conversationally, still lingering just *behind* the wheelchair, so his shadow was cast ominously over their suspect.

The old man, sitting in his chair, tried to twist at the neck to track Forester.

Forester said, "All those pretty young women. You never thought to chat one up? To see what other talents they might have? Never took it too far or anything?"

"Maybe you asked some of them to model for you," Artemis murmured quietly. "Maybe that's how it all started. Innocent enough. We understand that."

"Yeah, sure," said Forester. "Innocent. Ain't no crime in asking a pretty woman to pose for a painting, is there?"

Artemis and Forester were both staring at the pale-faced man.

He wasn't just nervous, though. He was also frightened. He kept glancing back and forth between the two of them, shaking his head, shivering horribly.

"I... I think you need to leave," he said slowly, his voice hoarse. "Now."

"I think you'd better tell us what's going on," Artemis shot back.

"You need to *leave*, now!" He yelled, spittle flying from his lips as he screamed at them. He waved a gnarled finger about like a baton now, pointing at Artemis and pointing at the door. "Get out! Get the hell out of my home!"

But Forester lowered his hand, resting it in a threatening manner on the old man's shoulder. Forester didn't squeeze, didn't do anything. He just left his hand there.

Mr. Faber swallowed, again bouncing his Adam's apple, and displaying a pronounced streak of white paint that had stained his wrinkled throat. He stared down at the hand on his shoulder, frozen in place, displaying a look of fear like someone who's spotted a spider on their arm.

Forester didn't move his hand. Mr. Faber didn't look away, save once, where his gaze darted longingly towards the shotgun on the couch.

Artemis glanced out the window once more, but there was no further sign of the dark-windowed sedan.

She looked back at Mr. Faber. "You were one of the four judges," she said softly. "For years, you were judging. Two of the years when Laura and Katya were in the competition..." She trailed off. "Do you know what happened to those girls?"

"No!" he said firmly. "You said disappeared. That's all I know. That sounds bad. Real bad. But no, I swear I don't."

"I think you do," Forester said conversationally. "I mean, hell, look at you, old man. Streaked in paint. Talking about hotties stripping down for your ogling pleasure. Mind you, I ain't judging. In a way, I'm congratulating. But you know. Anyone who was around that time—especially a painter—would know. Tell me you know, Faber. Look me in the eyes and tell me."

And now, Forester closed his hand. Not to squeeze. Not to cause pain. Just to remind the painter that the FBI agent was there. The calloused and scarred hand rested against the old man's naked shoulder.

And Faber began hyperventilating. He glanced back and forth between them, shaking his head. "I don't know shit. I don't."

"The Aristocrat," Forester said. "You know that name?"

"HELL NO!"

"You do."

"Get the hell out! Now!"

"You know the Aristocrat. Are you that guy? Were you once upon a time before you lost your vitality? Before you got stuck in this chair?"

"I don't know him, and I never met him! Now go away!"

Forester was glaring at the back of the old man's head. All the humor from before had vanished from Cameron's expression, and now his eyes were narrowed into slits. He was breathing slowly, and Artemis noticed the way his one hand had now tightened on the old man's shoulder. Forester's other hand fell to the back of the wheelchair, gripping it as well.

"You killed those women, didn't you?" Forester said, his voice hoarse. His eyes were wider now, it seemed, and his pupils dilated.

"Forester," Artemis said cautiously. "Cameron..."

But the old man was shaking his head violently. "I didn't do shit! Get out of my house! Get out!"

"Did you like watching them in pain? Did you like cutting them up, was that the fun part? Did you send taunting letters home? Huh?"

"What? What letters—no! Gross! No!"

"Forester," Artemis said cautiously, glancing towards the back of the house now. Her gaze fell on the patio door—a glass screen leading to the porch.

"We know you're a liar!" Forester yelled. "You killed her, didn't you! And you enjoyed it! Did you think I wouldn't find you? I wouldn't catch up, huh? I told you I would."

"You... what? I don't know you! HELP! Someone help!"

Forester began shaking the wheelchair now, violently. "Get up! I know you're faking it. Get the hell out of the chair. There's no ramp outside old man! We saw you moving around upstairs. STAIRS. Get it? Why the hell were you upstairs in a wheelchair! Get up! Get *up*!" Forester tilted the chair with a sudden heave.

One wheel lifted, and the old man spilled out with a shout.

Chapter 18

Artemis watched the scene play out in horror. She lunged forward, grabbing the old man under the arms and catching him before he hit the ground. His legs had buckled the instant Forester had attempted to dump him.

"Cameron!" Artemis yelled, grimacing as she held Mr. Faber aloft. "The back porch—*look*!"

Forester turned sharply while Artemis tried to push Faber back into his chair. The man was moaning now, shaking his head and saying, "Please—please don't hurt me! Alright! I'll tell you! You're psychos! What sort of monster does that!"

Forester was staring out the back window now, spotting what Artemis had moments before. A ramp.

Leading from the back porch, down to a rear entrance. The old man's front steps were in disrepair and didn't have a ramp because he didn't *use* them, not because he was faking an injury.

Artemis was murmuring, "I'm so sorry," again and again as she managed to heave Faber back into his chair.

Forester looked back, his face the same pale as Faber's. "I... I didn't..." he swallowed vaguely, frowning now. He looked down at his scarred hand, staring. He looked up again. "Upstairs..." he said faintly.

"I have an elevator, you idiot!" screamed Faber. "What the hell is wrong with you! Get out, please—oh, shit. No! NO, don't hurt me!"

Forester had stepped towards Artemis again, but now Faber was cringing in his chair, holding up a hand to protect his face.

For a moment, Artemis' insides wormed with guilt. She didn't like the way the old man was reacting to them. She didn't like feeling as if someone was so terrified of her that he thought she might hurt him for information.

Granted, Forester had made a mistake.

He'd thought Faber was faking the wheelchair. And also... something else. Something lingering in Cameron's eyes that she'd grown to recognize. A recollection—a haunted moment. PTSD, some called it.

Forester hadn't been fully *here*.

In fact, as she glanced at him, he still wasn't. The sociopath was breathing in and out heavily, his hands clenched at his sides. He didn't look like a jovial giant or mischievous partner anymore.

He just looked scary.

He looked dangerous.

His hands were opening and closing at his sides as he inhaled and exhaled shakily.

Artemis tried to calm him, murmuring, "It's okay," as she shot him quick looks. But at the same time, she needed information. Forester had set the stage.

SHE RUNS AWAY

Had scared their subject.

She wasn't proud of it. She didn't condone it, but what had been done was already done.

And she could *use* it.

No weapon wasted. Another one of Helen's favorite quotes. At the time, Artemis' older sister had been referring to the game of chess, but Artemis supposed that interrogations counted as well.

She said, quietly, "We don't *want* to hurt you, Mr. Faber. That is entirely up to you."

He stared at her, panicked now. He was no longer winking. At least there was that.

She kept her tone cold as ice, refusing to allow even a hint of compassion to creep into her voice. She said, quietly, "We just need you to tell us about the Aristocrat. By your reaction, we can tell you knew him."

"I didn't," he whispered. "I... I never did. But..." A moan. "He *said* I did. But I didn't!"

"Who said?" Artemis jumped on the comment, her heart pounding.

"The man..." A swallow. "The man who sent me the crate."

Artemis went stiff. "What? What crate?"

"No... no, please... I swore I wouldn't. I haven't. Please—is this a test? I didn't tell anyone! I swear. I swear on my mother's grave!" And now, Mr. Faber had lost all composure. Panic flared in his eyes, his nostrils widened and closed, and he was trembling horribly in his wheelchair, shaking his head side-to-side in rapid motions.

"I didn't! Just like he said. Do you work for him? Is that it?"

"Work for who?" Artemis asked.

"The Aristocrat! That psycho who sent me the crate! I didn't look. I never would've. I told you I didn't, please... *please,* go away!" He was moaning now, rocking back and forth and causing his wheelchair to creak.

Artemis just stared, frowning deeply. She shot a look at Cameron, but Forester was still breathing heavily, his face pale as he stared off into the distance.

"So someone came and gave you a crate... when was this?"

"Oh... I... twenty years ago?" he said suddenly, looking up. "Please," he murmured, his lips trembling, his forehead sweaty beneath his fisherman's cap. "I did what you asked. You said you wouldn't hurt me!"

"Did what *who* asked?" Artemis said. Then she shook her head. She knew who. The wrong question. "What did you do for the Aristocrat? How did you help him?"

Did she believe this? Was it an act? Was he confessing to some lesser thing in order to throw suspicion off himself? What if Mr. Faber really *was* the Aristocrat? What if he was in a wheelchair *now* but hadn't been thirty years ago? What if the wheelchair was the reason he'd mysteriously stopped his spree two decades ago?

She frowned as she considered all of this.

But that's when she glanced into the art studio. She stared at the painting on the easel, and then she knew.

An old, cartoon painting. A caricature of a nude woman. It wasn't *high* art. It wasn't very impressive at all.

And there, all across the wall, on either side of a mantelpiece, more paintings. All of them in the same style. Gaudy, bright colors. Paintings of baseball players or basketball stars or women in various states of undress.

Artemis was no purveyor of art, but she found the whole thing rather tasteless.

These were comic book characters... Not anything like the paintings that the Aristocrat had completed. She'd read online they'd used similar techniques. But the end product... entirely different.

And this man, sitting in a chair, shirtless, moaning. His house in disrepair, his yard a waste...

Was this the sort of man who'd paint masterpieces, and send them to museums to gain the attention of the world? Was this the sort of man who others called *the Aristocrat?*

No...

No, she didn't think so. The wheelchair, the artwork, the bearing... it was all too casual. This wasn't the killer. But he knew something.

And so, with severity, she snapped, "Tell me what you know, Jameson. What favor did you do for the Aristocrat?"

A whimper. Then, "I... I just helped him find the addresses of some girls. Some of the ones he liked. I didn't know at the time!" he added quickly. "I swear! I thought he was just a fan of the art. A collector who wanted to meet the girls. That was it!"

"I don't believe you!" Artemis yelled.

"I'm not lying! It was thirty years ago! Can't a man live his life! I didn't want to help. When I found out what was happening, I instantly stopped! I didn't want your stupid crate! It was all a horrible, horrible mistake. I didn't know what he was doing to those girls. I thought I was helping their careers!"

Now, Mr. Faber was shaking so badly that his chair rattled under him.

Artemis leaned in now, placing both hands on the armrests, staring Mr. Faber dead in the eyes. "You helped the Aristocrat choose his victims? You helped him find where they lived, by giving their personal information away? You had access... as a judge in the competitions, you had access."

"I didn't know..." A faint sob. "And I never gave anything about that poor fourth girl. By the first three, I realized what was happening. I'm stupid. I admit it. Dumb. But not evil. I made a mistake! I didn't know what he was doing."

"He paid you, didn't he?" Forester snapped from behind, having temporarily refocused it seemed.

Faber tried to turn to look in Forester's direction. He shivered, shaking his head as he turned. "It... it wasn't like that! He offered me an agent's fee. I deserved it, didn't I! No one was buying my work at the shows. No one! I was a judge, damn it! People didn't care! I just was trying to pay the bills. I thought I was helping those women's careers. If a collector picked up their pieces, it could mean the world to them! I was being *kind*!"

"And then you found out that three of the girls were dead," said Artemis. "And the fourth... you said you didn't give her name."

"Or the others! Any of the others," he said excitedly, with a tone like *ah-ha!* in his voice. "After I heard about the deaths, I got suspicious, and so I shut it down..."

"So how did he find his other victims?" Artemis said coldly.

"I don't know, but it wasn't me!"

A faint quiet fell over the room now, interrupted only by the rattle of Mr. Faber's wheelchair as he trembled in place. He was no longer glancing back and forth between them but had hunched over, breathing rapidly at his knees, his eyes closed as if in prayer.

Artemis stared at him. She felt a pang of sympathy, of sadness, of frustration.

She also found that she believed him.

She believed that this lonely old man had accepted bribes to give the personal information, phone numbers or addresses, of the contestants out to a stranger posing as a collector. Thirty years ago, such things would've been far harder to find online but far easier to distribute without oversight.

She also believed that there was more to the story.

She looked him in the eyes and said, "So what did he give you?"

Mr. Faber stared at the ground, refusing to meet her gaze, exhaustion now evident in his posture. He gave a small, sad shake of his head then sighed. "I never opened it," he repeated in that same small voice. And then, his shoulders slumped as if shriveled in on himself, he began to wheel down the hall.

He didn't gesture for them to follow, but Artemis did all the same.

Forester came along, both of them frowning after their retreating suspect.

The wheels in his chair creaked, and the old, faux-wooden floors joined the aching chorus. They reached a doorway in the wall, and Mr. Faber gestured towards it. He shook his head shakily. "I had the delivery men follow the instructions. It's down there. No one's ever touched it."

He glanced back at them, his gaze holding a haunted quality.

Artemis eased towards the door, her hand grazing the cold, brass handle. Forester stood in the hallway, just behind Mr. Faber. He nodded and said, "You wanna check. I can stay with our guest."

Artemis sighed slowly. The last time she'd entered a basement to examine some container, she'd discovered Fake Helen hiding in a trapped coffin.

She shivered, prickles rising along her skin.

But then she gave a quick nod towards Forester and pushed open the door. A set of old, dusty stairs led into the basement. Cobwebs covered the walls, and Artemis spotted more than one spider clinging to gossamer threads, dangling along the staircase. Were those black widows? She eyed the bulbous bodies of the arachnids with an air of extreme suspicion.

She edged along the concrete side of the staircase, attempting to avoid the spiders as much as possible. As she moved forward, cautiously, she listened to the sound of the creaking steps beneath her.

A gust of chill air swept up from the cold basement, sending prickles along her skin.

She glanced back over her shoulder, frowning in the direction of the two men.

They were like the subjects of some portrait, framed by the old doorway, both of them peering down after her. Faber's eyes held that same distant, haunted quality. Forester's expression was grim, attentive and watchful.

Artemis exhaled shakily.

Another step. The wood creaked. Another.

Crack.

Chapter 19

Artemis yelled in pain. Forester cried out. Faber gasped.

"Artemis!" Forester bellowed.

There was a surge of movement behind her, and Forester launched himself down the stairwell, taking six steps in one massive leap. He was at her side in an instant, like a guard dog responding to the command of its master.

Artemis, meanwhile, was wincing, massaging at her foot where she delicately extricated it from the stair it had smashed through.

"I'm fine!" she said, breathing heavily. "Old wood is all. I'm fine, Cameron."

Forester's nostrils flared, and he watched her with a look of extreme suspicion and doubt. But when she patted him on the arm and nodded back up the stairs, he frowned, double-checking her up and down. "You sure you're okay?" he said, his voice aching with concern.

She forced a quick smile, hiding her discomfort. A discomfort at how close the two of them were standing, sharing the same step now, just one below the shattered one. Their hands touching against the same rail for stability and support, his knuckles grazing hers.

She stared at his calloused fingers, swallowed, and looked up at him.

"I..." she trailed off. "I'm fine," she said at last, reorienting herself.

Just then, *wham!*

She turned sharply. Forester wheeled about as well and cursed. Faber had shut the door above them.

"God dammit," Cameron snapped. "He's gonna go for his shotgun."

Artemis stared at the door but neither of them moved towards it. Now the chance of a loaded double-barrel on the other side of that door cautioned both of their movements.

"We're not arresting him," she said with a shrug. "He's not the Aristocrat, anyway."

"I was thinking the same," Forester said after a moment, his voice a whisper.

He was still standing far, far too close for comfort. Artemis' mind felt fuzzy. Perhaps it was the cold, perhaps it was the anticipation of this mysterious *crate* in a basement. Something the Aristocrat had sent his old informant.

Was it true? Had Faber refused to open the crate for all these years?

Artemis shivered, her mind conjuring images of bones, old corpses, of trophies from his victims. Her mind spun with the possibilities, and she tried to quiet her racing thoughts.

There was a sudden sound of a sliding bolt. A shadow under the door. And then it disappeared.

"Well," Cameron muttered. "Guess he's not planning on killing us." He cursed. "Sorry. Shoulda stayed up there. I thought you were hurt."

She looked at him now, still standing on the same step, her hand still warmed by his. Temporarily, in the strangest way, it was as if she had tunnel vision. As if everything around her was forgotten. All she noticed, in that brief instance, was Forester standing next to her, watching her. The warmth of his breath against her cheek. The way his gaze fixated on her every twitch and motion as if reading her body like some sort of book.

It was strange, she thought, when the monster that went bump in the night also *cared*. Forester cared about her... He'd leapt halfway down the stairs because he cared.

He'd proven it again and again. Not just at the Dawkins residence, not just on the ranch... but now. He was standing by her. Not just literally, but *had* been at her side since this had all started.

Even while working for the agency, Forester had always played by his own rules...

But now?

Now he was toying with a conviction as an accomplice to double-homicide. He was playing with his freedom. And why?

Forester was still watching her. The sound of the rusted bolt sliding into place at the top of the stairs was forgotten.

The frigid cold breeze wafting up from the basement was also forgotten.

And now, the two of them faced each other, breathing softly, motionless. His tall frame seemed almost to dwarf hers, his shadow extending, resting on her. Her chin tilted ever so slightly, not quite meeting his gaze.

She studied his cheek, his nose, his mouth... his lips.

"Artemis..." Forester said slowly, his voice husky and soft. "I..."

She came to her senses in a jolt and shook her head. "Shit... we need to hurry." She pushed off his muscled chest, leveraging herself back down the stairs, avoiding the middle of the steps to avoid plunging her foot through another plank of old wood.

As she did, she felt a flush of embarrassment.

What the hell was that? She thought to herself, scathingly. They were on the clock. They were locked in a basement with an old man and his shotgun upstairs. Jamie and Sophie's lives were on the line.

And she was making eyes at the sociopathic federal?

Stupid. Idiot. Dumbass... The accusations came thick and fast, flooding her mind. She bunched her fists at her side as she emerged in the cold basement, standing in the unfinished, concrete room, peering across the ground.

Forester followed after her. She didn't look at him, and he remained off to her side.

He cleared his throat as if to speak again, but Artemis overrode him, saying, "There—that must be what he meant!"

Forester went quiet again.

The two of them stared at an old, wooden crate, yellowed with age, caked in dust and set under a window fifteen paces away.

The rest of the basement was sparsely furnished. Only a few shelves in one corner, with empty jars. Otherwise, the basement was empty. Like some prison cell.

A small window, stained and laden with dust, sat in the wall above the crate. Artemis briefly thought she glimpsed a flicker of shadow through the window, like someone moving outside the house, but then Forester spoke, "Twenty years he's had this, huh? Isn't that what he said?"

"Yeah... yeah, he said the Aristocrat sent this to him twenty years ago."

"And told him not to open it... why?"

Artemis shook her head, wondering just *how many* bodies might fit in that container. It was about the size of a chair. Rectangular and studded with nails securing the wooden beams in place.

She approached cautiously, her brow furrowed, her fingers reaching out and rubbing at the rough grain of the old wood.

Dust tumbled where she touched, and flecks of mealy wood fell away. There were no markings on the crate. No visible directions on how to open the thing.

Forester pointed low, though, and Artemis followed his gaze. A date was marked, just barely visible, in red ink staining the wood. "Huh," Forester said. "He wasn't lying. Twenty years ago. This thing has been down here for two decades."

"The same time the Aristocrat stopped his killing spree."

Forester and Artemis both breathed shakily, staring at the strange crate. The house had made creaking sounds earlier but now had fallen completely silent.

"You don't think..." Forester hesitated, then brushed past her, his motions cavalier, as if nothing had passed between them on those steps.

He peered down at the box, frowning. "You don't think maybe it's..."

"I hope not," Artemis cut in quickly. She wasn't sure what the end to that sentence would've been, but she also didn't *want* to know.

Forester nodded vaguely. His frown remained, and he reached out carefully, his fingers probing at the wooden crate.

Then, he shrugged.

It was like watching an engine rev to life. One moment, stooped, staring. The next, Forester's arms flung out. His fingers found purchase in gaps beneath the binding boards. And his arms strained. She watched the way his muscles bulged under the fabric of his shirt.

He was no longer wearing the suit he so often wore unbuttoned, or *mis*buttoned as was often the case.

Now, he simply wore a long-sleeve black, t-shirt, which emphasized the exertion he was putting into it. He tore the planks of wood free with a heavy gasp and flung the wood off to the side.

He rolled his shoulders and tore off another section of wooden braces. Then another.

The splinters rained down around him. Dust particles scattered on the air. For a brief moment, Artemis wondered if *this* was how Forester had looked while fighting professionally.

He almost appeared...

Unhinged.

Now, a box that had *never* had hinges, lay open. One large, wooden panel toppled as Forester pried it free from its loosed berth, and a large cloud of dust kicked up where the lid hit the ground.

The two of them waved hands in front of their faces, clearing the air, and, wincing, Artemis leaned in.

Bubble-wrap encircled a rectangular surface.

Forester tore this apart.

Then styrofoam. He ripped this as well.

Artemis just watched, mildly intimidated by the sheer, wanton destruction. Eventually, they were left with a single, dark rectangle sitting amidst a pile of debris. Foam, wood chips, nails and plastic wrap lay scattered around Forester's feet.

He was breathing heavily now and reached up to brush some of his hair back. He then glanced back at Artemis, his arms still straining under his shirt; he quirked an eyebrow. "Well?" he said.

She stepped closer, avoiding some of the discarded wood chips. The light through the streaked window in the wall settled on the item, illuminating it like some sort of spotlight.

A black, rectangular case with grooves on either end.

She approached, hesitantly.

"Is that what I think it is?" Forester murmured.

"It looks like it," Artemis replied.

They both nodded, and then she frowned. She didn't like that they were on the same wavelength, thinking the same thing without having to speak it out loud.

She shivered faintly and touched the case. It was only about an inch thick. About three feet in length.

It resembled a window.

Or…

A picture frame.

She pried at the box, like a shoe box, except much thinner and longer, one solid piece of cardboard slid over another.

The box made a faint squeaking sound as she slid it open. Forester was still watching her but had stationed himself with a perfect view of the stairwell and the window, just in case.

But her instincts had been correct. They weren't here for Mr. Faber—not if he wasn't the Aristocrat. If they arrested him, what then? Drive him around in the back of their car until he got suspicious that they weren't actually representing the FBI?

No...

They were here to find one man, and one man only.

A man who had disappeared twenty years ago.

Artemis opened the rectangular box fully now. No dust inside. It had been packed with such care and precision.

The care and precision of a man who *cared* deeply about the contents of the box. Sent to a stranger's house, kept in the basement for twenty years.

And as she allowed the lid of the tall, flat box to fall away, she found herself staring.

Forester let out a low whistle. "Damn," he murmured. "he really was good, wasn't he?"

Artemis just nodded, dumb and deaf.

The missing painting of the Aristocrat.

The eighth and final painting. The one supposedly tinged in Bella Doler's blood.

Like the other paintings she'd seen in evidence photographs, this one was masterfully crafted. The acrylic strokes almost seemed three-dimensional, with texture of their own. The figures and faces in the painting were so lifelike, they took Artemis' breath away.

She found herself gazing at the picture, her brow furrowed, her mouth threatening to unhinge until Forester nudged her.

She jolted at the touch, pulling her arm back as Forester said, "It isn't finished."

She stared at the painting, noticing the white, sketched portion in the bottom right corner. Most of the painting had been completed save this small, three-inch by three-inch square in the bottom right. In contrast to the dimensionality of the painted sections, it almost seemed *comical* the way a part of the canvas was blank save for the occasional pencil mark providing sketch lines of unfinished faces and feet.

"What is it, do you think?" Artemis asked quietly.

"Storming of the Bastille," Forester replied. "Start of the French Revolution. Buncha citizens tried to get weapons from an old prison, then someone fired a shot, probably a guard, and all hell broke loose. What? Why are you staring at me like that?"

"Just... How do you know that?" Artemis said, frowning.

Forester snorted. "I may look like a dumb jock with lumpy ears and stupid scars, but in reality... well... actually, that's probably all true. But I also know things. Sometimes." He shrugged.

"Have you been to Paris?"

Forester ignored this and just waved a hand back at the painting. "I mean, he's sticking with the eighteenth and nineteenth-century vibe. Why do you think that is?"

"I don't know. But this part of the painting is missing... he didn't finish it?"

Forester stared, leaning in. The sound of the wheelchair across creaking floorboards above was absent. The basement had fallen strangely and eerily silent.

Artemis' mind was whirring. She stared at the painting, briefly hesitant. "I don't... I don't understand why this is here? Why isn't it finished?"

"For twenty years it's been down here," Forester said.

"Exactly. Why did he send it to Mr. Faber at all? Why did..." A loud creak on the floor above, and Artemis went quiet, staring up. She frowned and waited a moment, but when no further sounds were forthcoming, she dropped her voice to a whisper and continued, "This was the Aristocrat's life's work... *Who* was he?" Artemis trailed off, hesitating only briefly.

"What is it?" Forester said, studying the side of her face. "What's the matter."

"Just..." Artemis murmured, hesitated, then said, "I... something about this painting..." She wrinkled her nose, tilting her head to the side, still staring at the portrait. "It isn't finished."

"So?"

"Do you see any red, here?"

"No... why?"

"No blood."

"Well, I mean... it was mixed in, wasn't it?"

"Yes, but he painted with the blood. Without mixing it. In all his other paintings, there were streaks of red—the blood of his victims."

"So?"

"No blood," Artemis repeated, pointing at the white canvas. She stared at the empty portion of the painting and then tapped a finger against the unpainted section. "What do those look like?"

"Umm... an arm. Flowers?"

"What type of flowers."

"Roses... Red roses," Forester said. "So you think he was *going* to paint this with blood... So why didn't he?"

"Why not indeed?" Artemis replied.

And now, as she stared at the painting, she could feel a faint prickle climbing up her spine. "I'm missing something," she whispered softly.

Forester was still shooting glances back to the stairs, making sure they were still safe.

"I mean... the Aristocrat was a vindictive murderer. I don't think we can expect to *understand* why he did what he did."

"No... no, maybe..." She trailed off then glanced sharply at Forester. "What did you say?"

"I... I don't think we can expect—"

"No! Before that!"

"I said... the Aristocrat was a vindictive murdere—"

"He was... wasn't he? Vindictive."

Forester's cheeks puffed with air and he exhaled deeply. "I'm not sure what you're driving at. Artemis? Hey—Artemis, what is it?"

But she was staring at the painting again. An unfinished painting. No blood. Why was there no blood? Unless... "These paintings would've taken *ages* to complete, right?"

"Yeah, so?"

"So... his first victim. Katya Solenger. She was taken, then two weeks later the painting was released."

"And?"

"He couldn't have finished the painting in two weeks."

"Huh. I mean... yeah, you're right. So what does that mean?"

Artemis was shaking her head, pacing now, glancing around the room as if seeing everything clearly for the first time. She felt the prickle along her spine now spreading to her arms, along the tips of her fingers. She said, slowly, "I think... I think it means that the Aristocrat *started* his painting *long* before he kidnapped Katya." She then pointed at *this* particular painting. "And the same could be said of this one."

"I don't understand?"

"Why not just finish it? Why send it here at all?"

Forester just watched her, clearly deciding it was better to listen in this moment than contribute.

Artemis was pacing more rapidly, a few pieces of styrofoam fluttered away as she did. She was wagging a finger up and down as she strode back and forth. "Only that small section left. All he needed was blood."

"So?"

"What if he didn't have any?" Artemis said, looking sharply at Forester.

Cameron blinked. "I'm... not following."

"What if he didn't have any blood?"

"But... he kidnapped Bella Doler. The warden's daughter."

"Did he?"

"Well... *yes*. Didn't he? She was the same type as the other girls. Pretty, young, an artist. It was in the papers."

"But why was it?" Artemis asked. She hesitated, closing her eyes and cycling back through her memory, examining all the articles she'd read concerning the Aristocrat and his crimes.

The words flew across her mind. The images and text and headlines like screenshots, flitting through her memory. She paused occasionally, studying intently. And then said, "Anonymous sources."

"Excuse me?"

She opened her eyes, staring at Forester. And now, the prickles along her spine intensified. Something was wrong. She'd missed something. Something that should've been obvious. She said, "An anonymous source tipped the newspapers that the Aristocrat was the culprit behind Bella Doler's disappearance."

"I don't understand."

"She was the right type. The right age. The right interests. The right area..." Artemis trailed off. "But an anonymous source confirmed it... Holy shit."

"What?"

"HOLY SHIT!"

"Artemis, *what*?"

She stared at the painting, her eyes the size of coins, her heart hammering a million miles per second. Her jaw felt as if it wanted to fall off and rest near her toes. She just shook her head, gaping now. "God... No blood, Forester. There's no *blood*!" She pointed with a tremoring finger at the painting.

It all made sense now.

Small clues... breadcrumbs, really. A trail she never could've found if not for the crumbs. But they led back to an inevitable conclusion.

One that baffled her. It didn't make sense at first, but as it settled in her mind, like the final moves against a chess engine, she realized that standard lines wouldn't work here.

No... The truth was written so *clearly* it nearly brought her to her knees.

"I've got it..." Artemis whispered. "I know who the Aristocrat is... well. No. I know *how* to find him."

"How?"

But just then, a loud sound of thumping. Protesting. *BAM!* A gunshot and then yelling.

"On the ground—get on the ground! FBI!" snapped a loud voice.

Forester and Artemis whirled to stare at the door at the top of the basement. The voice was coming from further in the house though.

"Was that a..."

"Gunshot," Forester said. Then he cursed, "That's Wade's voice. Shit... *shit!*"

"Your partner? Desmond Wade?"

"YES!"

Chapter 20

Artemis stared at Cameron, her eyes round. "But... but that's not..."

"Ms. Blythe?" A voice called out from above now. "Desmond, please cuff that man... kick the shotgun away. Cameron?"

"That's auntie!" Forester said, his voice rising an octave. "Shit—*shit!* We have to go!"

"How? They're upstairs!" Artemis felt her blood pressure increasing. She should've known—the car with the tinted windows outside. The shadow behind the window... Supervising Agent Shauna Grant and Special Agent Desmond Wade had found them.

Had they come with backup?

No...

There was a smashing sound. And Artemis whirled to find Forester clearing glass from the window. He made a stirrup out of his hands, resting them against his knee, and nodding down.

Artemis didn't need a second invitation. Faint rays of sunlight poked through the opening in the wall. She shielded her eyes with an upraised hand and hastened forward, pushing off Cameron's leg, and rising towards the glass. Her long-sleeved shirt fell over her palms, protecting her as she crossed to the ground, clearing the glass. And then she wriggled through the smashed window.

Behind her, she heard the sound of the door at the top of the stairs being opened.

Now, as she emerged, the sounds grew fainter. Old, overgrown grass tickled her face, her cheek. In a way, it disguised her, the knee-length grass rising higher than her prone form.

She crawled through, wriggling desperately. Her elbows gouged into the ground. She heard footsteps against the stairs.

And when she glanced back, Forester hadn't followed.

A second too late, she realized the window was too damn small for the broad-shouldered ex-fighter.

She stared, cursing.

Forester was looking out at her, his expression severe. "Go!" he whispered at her. And then he flung the car keys through the window. They indented the grass, bending long stalks.

Artemis stared, cursed, snatched the keys and spun on her heel, breaking into a sprint.

She heard shouting now.

Forester's voice. Then Desmond's. Then the voice of someone else—backup, most likely.

She rounded the side of the old, dilapidated home but came to a stumbling halt. Breathing heavily, she stared towards the curb. Two cops were standing by her car, both chatting casually. Six more cop cars were pulling down the street.

Three police officers were now moving around the house, towards where she was peeking out. One of the officers was gesturing at the others. "Window in the back," he was saying. "Agent Grant wants sentries. Shit—hurry up, we're late." This last comment was prompted by more shouting from inside the house.

Then more gunshots.

Artemis stiffened, her spine tingling.

Was Forester alright?

Was Wade? Who'd fired the shots?

Everything was collapsing around her. She was alone. Forester was captured. And three cops were now twenty paces away, moving past the front facade of the house, along the side, heading straight towards her.

"Shit... shitshitshit," she cursed with a sputtering sound like a motorboat. More voices. This time behind her.

She glanced back, and spotted more cops, emerging from the fence line *behind* the house. Two more officers, both of them staring towards the back window, pointing.

"Hey!" one of them shouted. "Someone came out the back!"

The three cops approaching Artemis frowned and then broke into a jog, the flashlights and weapons at their utility belts clattering as their shiny, black boots shimmered against the long blades of grass.

So Artemis did the only thing she could think of.

She wasn't a fighter. She couldn't take on three assailants the way Forester did.

And in this instance, she had to take a shot.

So she went low.

First, she stepped back, still in the shadow of the house, hiding behind the frame.

Then, listening to the voices behind her, examining the window, just a foot out of sight. If either of those cops took a step to the right, they'd see directly along the house and spot her. But for now, they were staring at the shattered glass of the back window facing the backyard.

She heard the running footsteps of the cops from the front yard, coming straight towards her.

And so she dropped.

The grass was tall. *Very* tall. Completely untended, already turning to seed and fluttering above her. At knee height, her thin form was covered by the overgrown lawn.

She wedged herself against the house, prone, laying low, in the shadows. The stalks of grass rustled above her, and she tried to pull some of the blades to obscure her head.

The human head, she felt, was the portion of a body that would be spotted easiest.

And then she closed her eyes, facing the dust, not wanting the reflection in her gaze to attract anyone's attention, nor for subconscious motions caused by movement to redirect her gaze. She lay there, in the shadow of the old house, wearing her usual black sweater, her thin form swaddled by the tall, jutting grass.

And she waited and listened.

The footsteps hastened past her. Panting breaths left her in their wake.

"Everything okay down there?" someone was shouting. "Shit—shots fired!"

SHE RUNS AWAY

Artemis lay motionless, panicked and scared. She listened for further sounds. Waited. Quiet and cautious. More shouts, still from the backyard.

"HOLY SHIT—HE'S GOT MY LEG! HELP!"

The bloodcurdling scream went quiet a second later, following the sound of a dull *thump*.

Artemis chose this moment to move.

She didn't bolt, but instead walked casually, strolling forward as she did, not wanting to gain any attention. She didn't emerge around the front of the house, but—glancing side to side and finding the coast clear—she hopped the fence leading into the neighbor's yard.

No one called after her. The only sounds were coming from the backyard.

Forester, by the sound of things, was putting up a fight. Ten against one, and he was still going. The gunshots had stopped, and she hoped no one had been hurt.

Artemis shot a glance back over her shoulder, peering through the branches of a low-hanging tree. Faint motion in the front yard.

But she couldn't stop. There was nothing she could do to help.

Jamie Kramer was still on a timer.

And so she broke into a sprint, keeping along the sides of the old homes. Using the fact that the houses were set back on the lots, hidden behind old trees and tangled vegetation. She ran, surging away from the scene of the crime.

The Aristocrat's painting remained behind her.

Forester remained behind.

Mr. Faber, the man who'd claimed he'd unwittingly *helped* the Aristocrat, remained behind.

And Artemis kept going, along the houses, her phone now emerging in a trembling hand. She needed to make a call. A call she'd never placed before.

She raised the phone, hand still shaking, breathing heavily.

Was she right?

It was what made sense. The *only* thing that put *all* the pieces together. She had to use all the pieces—that was the only way.

And only one picture fit everything together.

Quick glances through the trees along the side of the road kept her attentive. A few neighbors were sitting on the porch off to her left, staring at her, dumbfounded. She stared back then quickly smiled and nodded. She waved a hand over her shoulder, "See what's happening at Faber's? Crazy, right?"

Casually, she kept moving.

The neighbors on the porch just stared after her then turned, frowning in the direction of the flashing cop cars.

She kept going, and only once she'd reached the end of the block did the phone lift to her ear.

She paused, remembering the number she'd memorized.

Then placed the call.

Three rings.

Then someone answered.

She waited through the preamble and said, "I need to speak to the warden."

A pause.

"Tell him I know who killed his daughter."

A reply.

She said, "And also…" she hesitated, "Tell him I found the Aristocrat. I know who it is. At least… I *will* know very soon. Tell him to call me back."

She hung up and kept moving.

She waited, and then placed another call, this time for a taxi. Sirens wailed in the distance. But she stood off on the side of the road, under dark treetops, trembling and shivering as her call connected to the taxi service.

The receptionist at the prison must have transferred the message quickly.

Because no more than a few minutes passed before Artemis' phone began to ring.

She lifted the device, swallowing once.

She waited, answered.

A pause. A polite, careful, cautious voice. "Who is this, please?"

"Mr. Doler… I know who the Aristocrat is, sir. The man who killed your daughter. I'm going to tell you everything, but I need a favor in return. Listen *very* closely."

Chapter 21

It was dark by the time Artemis pulled into the parking lot in the Easter Lake Forest Preserve. Fifteen minutes from Pinelake and thirty-five minutes from her father's prison.

She stepped out of the taxi and waited for the driver to pull away before turning and glancing at the only other car in the parking lot.

Raindrops had *just* started to tumble from the skies.

Artemis swallowed faintly, wetting cracked lips, and staring at the car with the headlights on. A dark sedan, tinted windows.

She glanced back, waiting for the taxi to disappear, and then she turned to face the car.

The front door to the vehicle opened.

A man got out.

A man in a gray suit. He had neatly parted, choir-boy hair. A small goatee—pure white—and eyebrows two shades darker.

He looked like a distinguished schoolteacher. Or perhaps a defense attorney. Which, in fact, was exactly what he *had* been before becoming a warden. Wasn't that what Artemis had recalled when speaking to Mrs. Doler earlier that day?

She exhaled shakily, staring at Carmin Doler. The warden of her father's prison.

He stood by the front of his car, blinking a couple of times owlishly, his features illuminated by the glow.

Artemis stared right at him.

She hadn't invited Mrs. Doler. Not this time. Everything was clear now—*no*. For this to work, Mrs. Doler couldn't be here.

Artemis stepped forward, anxiety swirling in her stomach.

She stared at the man by the car, watching him, shivering. "You came!" she called out, trying to conceal the excitement, the nerves in her voice.

He watched her closely, nodding once.

"My wife told me about you," he said quietly. "Artemis Blythe. I know your father."

She blinked. His wife had told him? That didn't make sense.

She said, "Your wife didn't tell you anything. It was one of your nephews."

He watched her. Then nodded. "You're like him. Clever?"

She shook her head. Now, the rain was picking up, falling faster. "I'm not like him at all," she said.

The two of them stood in the forest preserve's parking lot, watching each other attentively. Fifteen paces away, the length of a couple of cars. The warden's car was still running, the lights illuminating her.

"It's my wife, isn't it?" Doler said simply. "She's involved somehow."

Artemis just watched him. "Do you have what I asked for?"

"You first," he said.

"I wasn't sure, you know," she replied, shaking her head. "An innocent man wouldn't have shown up. He would've sent cops. I was watching from back there." She waved a hand over her shoulder, across the river, towards one of her favorite hang-out spots from when she'd been a child. Tommy, Helen and Artemis had fished in that river many a time. There was a perfect lookout spot. She had watched...

Not for long, though. The taxi had kept the meter running at the vehicle entrance, so she'd only had a few minutes.

But it had been long enough to guarantee that the warden had come alone. She waved a hand, blinking against the headlights. Small droplets of scattering rain were illuminated by the glow.

She pointed at the warden. "But you came."

He didn't move. Then he snorted. "You think I'm the Aristocrat?"

"No," she said, shaking her head.

"Then what's this about? You said you knew *who* the Aristocrat was. You said you knew what happened to my daughter."

"And you came," she said. "On something as scant as that. It confirmed what I thought. You being here."

The warden snorted and turned, reaching for his car door. "I don't have to listen to this."

"If you kill me," she continued as if he hadn't said anything—which he hadn't, not really. It was all a bluff. "I have three friends ready to release the information to your wife, to the DA, to the police and to the press. If they don't hear back from me and see me on video, they'll do it."

This wasn't true either. She'd only told Tommy. But as far as backup was concerned, in the right state of mind, Tommy was as good as three men.

The warden turned away from his car now, staring at her. "What do you want?"

"I told you."

"And we can get to that. What do you *know?*"

"Only what you've confirmed for me here," she replied.

The drizzle had turned to raindrops. Her clothing was now cold. Damn. Portions were now being plastered to her skin. She glared back at the warden, allowing the pieces to fit together once more in her mind. Yes... a nephew had told him.

Not the wife.

The wife had suspected her husband. Not of being the Aristocrat. Of course not...

But she'd wanted leverage.

Wasn't that what she'd said? "*My husband is a vindictive man... he wants to take the house in the proceedings... But, we'll handle this my way.*"

The comment had seemed so innocuous at the time. But everything hinged on it.

"Mrs. Doler loved your daughter," Artemis said quietly. "She really, really did. Didn't she?"

The warden just stared at her, motionless, frozen in place.

"You did as well."

"Go to hell. Really... this... I'm not standing for this. You don't know anything, do you? You're just fishing."

"I've caught what I wanted. I have. Truly. The fish came to meet me. Alone. No cops. No backup. You're alone. Not because you didn't think you needed backup. But because you want to kill me. Just like you did with the Aristocrat."

He stared at her.

Didn't look away. Didn't protest fast enough. Too slow.

Another piece slotted into place.

She continued before he could object, "I was trying to figure out why there was no blood in that painting. And then I realized... Because the Aristocrat *never* took your daughter."

The old, distinguished-looking warden didn't look so distinguished now, but he did look old. "What are you talking about?" he demanded.

"The Aristocrat didn't take her. Bella Doler. Your daughter. I saw a picture, you know. Your wife standing close to her. I thought it was because your wife loved her. And she did. But there was a secret. A secret your daughter told your wife. I thought it was your wife's secret. But it was the other way around. And your wife had long suspected it, Mr. Doler. But she didn't *truly* know." Artemis spoke coldly, clinically. She didn't stop. She kept going. Now, the rain had picked up. The trees were rustling around them.

The river behind them sloshed against the banks. Artemis said, continuing in a slow, dull cadence like a funeral dirge. "Your wife didn't love your daughter more. At least, that's not what I kept seeing in the photos. It was that your daughter feared you more. Because of what you'd been doing to her. With her. Isn't that true, Mr. Doler?"

Now he exploded. The calm facade vanished. His face turned red. He began shouting, yelling, "Are you insane, you absolute swine! I never touched her! *Never*! How *dare* you! I loved my daughter!"

"Yes... In the wrong way. I know what you did, and so do you. I'm not here to convince you. Here's my phone—see, not recording. Would you like me to pull up my shirt so you can see I'm not wearing a wire? Or would that tempt you, too much? The same way your daughter did, twenty years ago."

"You're insane," he muttered.

"But you're still standing *right* there. You didn't lunge at me. You didn't pull that gun I know is in your..."

She trailed off as the weapon suddenly emerged.

He pointed it at her, glaring darkly. His hand was shaking horribly. He swallowed.

"You killed your daughter, sir," Artemis said quietly, completely indifferent to the gun. She hadn't come here to preserve her own life. She'd come here to save Jamie's. And so she kept marching, refusing to look back. "You killed your daughter so she wouldn't tell anyone what you'd been doing with her. Didn't you?"

No blood on the painting. Because there was no victim. Because the Aristocrat had *sent* his painting before he'd finished it.

Why? That was the question. *Why?*

And the answer had been obvious. Everything fell into place. It all made sense now.

The slick weapon in the warden's hand only confirmed what she'd suspected. He'd confirmed it by arriving. It had been one of two things. Maybe three, but the third had been an outlier and had involved Mrs. Doler.

But this?

No... *this* was the truth.

"In a way, Mrs. Doler suspected something, didn't she?" Artemis asked quietly. "She wanted me to look into it because she wanted leverage in the divorce. But I don't think even she knows what you did.

I think she knows about the *second* person you killed. Or... at least... *had* killed. But if she knew you'd done that to your own daughter—"

"Quiet now," said the man. And though his voice was strained, he spoke with an air of authority. "You're a fugitive from the law, Artemis Blythe. Hands in the air."

She shook her head. "I'm not recording you. No one is watching. It's just the two of us."

"Hands in the air!" he snapped through gritted teeth.

"Shoot me," she said softly, "and everyone will know. Every single person. We found the Aristocrat's missing painting, by the way. He shipped it to an old acquaintance for safekeeping. I had to ask myself *why* did he do that." She didn't even look at the gun, preferring to stare the man dead in the eyes.

"And why is that?" he snapped.

"Because," she said simply, "he thought he'd get it back. He'd continue his little game. Kidnap more, kill more. The Aristocrat was a very *real* killer. But you knew that, didn't you?"

"He killed my daughter."

"No, he didn't. He was one of your clients, wasn't he? I looked back on my drive here. Around the same time that the Aristocrat disappeared, a man named Boone Gentry was arrested." She gave a morbid chuckle. "Gentry. That was his last name. Imagine that."

"Boone, who?"

"Oh, you remember him. You were his defense attorney. He was arrested on stalking charges—breaking a restraining order, wasn't he? A young woman... Someone who was pretty, in her teens and... a painter, right? But no one knew what he *really* was. No one except... his lawyer." She raised her eyebrows staring at the warden. "You were

SHE RUNS AWAY

once a defense attorney. I remembered that while speaking with your wife. And Boone Gentry was your client. Did he tell you? Did you figure it out? When did it occur to you that you could use the Aristocrat's legacy as a trap? You *knew* Boone was going away for a year."

She was nodding as she spoke. "It all makes sense. He shipped that unfinished painting to an old friend because he thought he would be coming back for it in a year. But that's not what happened, was it?"

"What do you mean?" the warden was glassy-eyed now, frozen in place. Water droplets streaked his features. This was a guilty man.

A very guilty man. His stench was the brimstone odor of sin.

She let out a fluttering sigh. "Your wife said you were a vindictive man, but she didn't know the half of it. The Aristocrat did *not* have another victim. Which was why the painting was unfinished. He didn't have the blood. Didn't have your daughter. Which only means someone *else* killed your daughter. Then, I remembered the photos—how far Bella stood from you. She feared you. Your wife hates you. It makes sense. People aren't so hard to read as most think. And see, if the Aristocrat didn't kill Bella, then I had to look at it another way. I didn't know. And then you came here. You came alone. You came with a gun. And now it's pointing at my head. You have no intention of arresting me. You would've called the police by now. I'm unarmed. See?" she turned slowly, side to side. "No weapons."

"Hands up," he snarled.

"You confirmed it, sir. You killed your daughter because you slept with her. And then you spoke with a man named Boone Gentry and found out who he was. Perhaps he bragged, trusting attorney-client privilege. Or perhaps you intuited his guilt, you clearly are a clever man."

"Stop!"

"You won't shoot me," she said simply. "You would've already. But you know I'm telling the truth. Everything will be ruined for you. You don't care about me. You care about your reputation. And I," she said slowly, and in a way, this was the hardest part, "Am not here to get you in trouble. No one has to know."

She let the words settle. Spat off to the side, rainwater accumulating on her lips.

He stared at her, and she didn't look away.

"So what do you want then?" he snapped.

"Tell me," she said quietly, "Did you have Boone Gentry killed in prison yourself? Did someone do it as a happy accident? You used him as a scapegoat. You used him as the perfect red herring. You killed your daughter, then used your client, Mr. Gentry, to take the fall. No one knew who the Aristocrat was. And so the Aristocrat disappeared. For twenty years. His unfinished painting has been collecting dust for twenty years. Jameson Faber has been living in fear, sitting on the crate of a dead man. A man you had killed in prison." She then recited from memory. "Recent stabbing in the showers at Backenridge Correctional Facility. One casualty. Boone Gantry." She shook her head. "They even got his name wrong. Gantry. An obscure, one-line death for a man who wanted fame more than anything. He was stabbed, his blood left on the shower floors. Like paint."

She stared at the warden and didn't move an inch. She stood rigid, back to the entrance to the forest preserve.

Fearless. Motionless, glaring.

"When did your career shift from defense attorney to warden?" she said softly. "You were briefly a prison guard, I noticed. In fact, you applied for the position only a *month* after Mr. Gentry was sentenced. I wonder why that is... Don't you?"

And then the silence fell.

The raindrops, the stirring trees, the rushing river, all seemed to quiet as if shushed by some greater presence. Something watching from the sky.

Something thick and heavy on the air.

Artemis didn't look away. She just held the gaze of the warden, water flecking her features. And then, her chest twisting, she said quietly, "I'm going to make you an offer. I promised you the information as a trade. I will stick to my promise. It isn't in my nature to let a man like you flee, but I have others I need to care for, and as far as I can tell, you've never killed another." She shook her head, the guilt lancing through her, but she ignored it.

"You've made it all up," the warden sneered. "None of it is true. You can't prove any of it."

"I don't have to. I don't want to. You don't need that gun. You won't use it. It can't stop the information from being released, from ruining your life... One bullet in me is as good as one in you. The public humiliation, your wife getting everything... the truth about what you did to your own flesh and blood. Your own daugh—"

"Enough!" he screamed. "Fine. So what... I give you what you want and..."

"And I let you walk free."

"I don't believe you."

She nodded. "What choice do you have, sir? You've lived with a secret for twenty years. You've developed a thick skin. Move to France. Change location. I don't care. I'll keep my word. I don't want to. I want you in jail. I want the truth out... but I want something else even more."

A flash of kind eyes. Of an honest face. She exhaled faintly, thinking of the ranch, of Sophie's small, pink lunchbox.

And there was only one way to get *any* of that.

The warden breathed slowly. "You won't tell a soul?"

"No."

"And if you do," he said, his voice cold, "I'll have someone kill you. I know people, Artemis Blythe." Now, he seemed to have gotten over his fear that she was recording, that cops were waiting in the bushes. Sheer hatred emanated from his gaze. The hatred of a man who'd seared his conscience so fully there was no recovery apart from divine intervention.

But... a man like this? Had he ever had a functioning conscience?

He pointed his gun at the ground now, trembling, his white goatee soaked from the raindrops. He said, "If you release that information, I'll have them torture you first. Then kill you. I know people, and I have money. Believe me, Artemis Blythe. Not just you but everyone you love."

She shivered, staring at the sadistic man.

But she didn't let him see her fear. Instead, she shrugged and said, "I have a gun to your head, you have one to mine. Mutually assured destruction."

He hesitated then nodded. "As long as we understand each other."

"We don't. Not yet. First, you give me what I asked for. *Then* and only then will I keep my lips sealed. No one will know. No one can find out."

He just shrugged. "We have a deal, then," he said simply. And there was no shift in his voice. No change in his posture. The same eyes, the same tone as when he'd first arrived. Some killers had alter egos, hid their true natures.

But this man... a man who ran a prison, who could control lives and souls with his whim... *this* man didn't have to hide what he was.

And he smiled now, staring at her, water pouring down his features. In a way, his slick goatee almost looked like the curling chin horn of some devil.

"Deal then," she replied, and she felt sick doing it. But this man wasn't a threat to more lives... except her own. And she *had* no loved ones. None, really. None he could find. No family. No husband. No children. No parents. None except for the ones still missing.

The only person she cared for was in the clutches of a psychotic kidnapper. And this was the only path to free him.

So she said, her voice shaking, "We need to arrange a meet-up. How will you bring him to me, then?"

"Oh? I brought him already. Ms. Blythe," said the warden simply. "There's something you *don't* know about me, clever one, hmm? Always come with the carrot... *and the stick.*" He holstered his weapon and then stepped backwards. The locks to his vehicle clicked, and he opened the door to the back seat.

He turned to her, sending the door swinging wide with a flourish, like a magician presenting something on stage. He watched her with a grin as he did it, clearly wanting her to *see* what he was doing.

Wanting her to know the power he had.

And it *was* power. He was a warden but not without oversight. She'd known there were corrupt guards in that facility. Known there were people looking the other way. But now, the evidence that the corruption went far deeper than she'd known, was presented plain before her.

A man emerged from the vehicle, blinking raindrops, shivering and adjusting the casual suit he wore. The same suit, in fact, he'd been arrested in—half dressed. He was missing a tie. And his shoes were old, weathered loafers.

Artemis' heart pounded.

She stared, completely taken off guard.

Otto Blythe, the Ghost Killer, emerged from the back seat of the warden's car, a free man. Standing by the warden, staring at Artemis, a smile twisting his cheeks.

WHAT IS NEXT FOR ARTEMIS BLYTHE?

SHE ONCE DISAPPEARED

Artemis Blythe is on the run with only a convicted serial killer as an ally.

In order to rescue the man she loves, chessmaster and FBI agent Artemis has to perform a task for the man she hates. The Ghost-killer's demand is simple: find Helen.

Artemis' sister has been missing for nearly twenty years, long thought dead. And now, in order to appease her father and his accomplice, Artemis must discover what happened to Helen Blythe all those years ago.

Once upon a time, she'd thought the Ghost-killer had murdered his own daughter.

But new evidence is found, and Artemis is no longer so certain... The truth, it turns out, is far more bone-chilling.

ALSO BY GEORGIA WAGNER

GIRL UNDER THE ICE

Once a rising star in the FBI, with the best case closure rate of any investigator, Ella Porter is now exiled to a small gold mining town bordering the wilderness of Alaska. The reason for her

new assignment? She allowed a prolific serial killer to escape custody.

But what no one knows is that she did it on purpose.

The day she shows up in Nome, bags still unpacked, the wife of the richest gold miner in town goes missing. This is the second woman to vanish in as many days. And it's up to Ella to find out what happened.

Assigning Ella to Nome is no accident, either. Though she swore she'd never return, Ella grew up in the small, gold mining town, treated like royalty as a child due to her own family's wealth. But like all gold tycoons, the Porter family secrets are as dark as Ella's own.

Want to know more?

Greenfield press is the brainchild of bestselling author Steve Higgs. He specializes in writing fast paced adventurous mystery and urban fantasy with a humorous lilt. Having made his money publishing his own work, Steve went looking for a few 'special' authors whose work he believed in.

Georgia Wagner was the first of those, but to find out more and to be the first to hear about new releases and what is coming next, you can join the Facebook group by copying the following link into your browser - www.facebook.com/GreenfieldPress.

GEORGIA WAGNER

ABOUT THE AUTHOR

Georgia Wagner worked as a ghost writer for many, many years before finally taking the plunge into self-publishing. Location and character are two big factors for Georgia, and getting those right allows the story to flow seamlessly onto the page. And flow it does, because Georgia is so prolific a new term is required to describe the rate at which nerve-tingling stories find their way into print.

When not found attached to a laptop, Georgia likes spending time in local arboretums, among the trees and ponds. An avid cultivator of orchids, begonias, and all things floral, Georgia also has a strong penchant for art, paintings, and sculptures. A many-decades long passion for mystery novels and years of chess tournament experience makes Georgia the perfect person to pen the Artemis Blythe series.

More Books By Steve Higgs

Blue Moon Investigations
Paranormal Nonsense
The Phantom of Barker Mill
Amanda Harper Paranormal Detective
The Klowns of Kent
Dead Pirates of Cawsand
In the Doodoo With Voodoo
The Witches of East Malling
Crop Circles, Cows and Crazy Aliens
Whispers in the Rigging
Bloodlust Blonde – a short story
Paws of the Yeti
Under a Blue Moon – A Paranormal Detective Origin Story
Night Work
Lord Hale's Monster
The Herne Bay Howlers
Undead Incorporated
The Ghoul of Christmas Past
The Sandman
Jailhouse Golem
Shadow in the Mine
Ghost Writer

Felicity Philips Investigates
To Love and to Perish
Tying the Noose
Aisle Kill Him
A Dress to Die For
Wedding Ceremony Woes

Patricia Fisher Cruise Mysteries
The Missing Sapphire of Zangrabar
The Kidnapped Bride
The Director's Cut
The Couple in Cabin 2124
Doctor Death
Murder on the Dancefloor
Mission for the Maharaja
A Sleuth and her Dachshund in Athens
The Maltese Parrot
No Place Like Home

Patricia Fisher Mystery Adventures
What Sam Knew
Solstice Goat
Recipe for Murder
A Banshee and a Bookshop
Diamonds, Dinner Jackets, and Death
Frozen Vengeance
Mug Shot
The Godmother
Murder is an Artform
Wonderful Weddings and Deadly Divorces
Dangerous Creatures

Patricia Fisher: Ship's Detective Series
The Ship's Detective
Fitness Can Kill
Death by Pirates
First Dig Two Graves

Albert Smith Culinary Capers
Pork Pie Pandemonium
Bakewell Tart Bludgeoning
Stilton Slaughter
Bedfordshire Clanger Calamity
Death of a Yorkshire Pudding
Cumberland Sausage Shocker
Arbroath Smokie Slaying
Dundee Cake Dispatch
Lancashire Hotpot Peril
Blackpool Rock Bloodshed
Kent Coast Oyster Obliteration
Eton Mess Massacre
Cornish Pasty Conspiracy

Realm of False Gods
Untethered magic
Unleashed Magic
Early Shift
Damaged but Powerful
Demon Bound
Familiar Territory
The Armour of God
Live and Die by Magic
Terrible Secrets

Printed in Great Britain
by Amazon